Pixel Paradox

Pixel Paradox

THE LUMATORE CHRONICLES

T. Penyor Reed

Davlor Press

To my wife, Christine, who has always
believed in me, even when I didn't believe
in myself.

The Shifting Tundra
Ember Peaks
Azure Archipelago
Binaural Divide
Emberstone
Shadevale
Whispering Wood
Mystertop Peaks
Lumoran Plains
Enigma Expanse
(Uncharted)
City of Lumora
Silverleaf
Mists of Iseldar
Rosewater Bay
Village

One

Nexxus

Alex Porter was a presence that blended into the crowd. His appearance, while unremarkable at first glance, held subtle nuances that made him unique in his own right. He looked considerably younger than his 28 years, though his thoughtful hazel eyes betrayed his youthful appearance.

He had a medium build, neither too tall nor too short, standing at around 5 feet 10 inches. His fair complexion occasionally bore the faintest freckles across the bridge of his nose during the summer months. His hair was a shade of medium brown, cut in a simple, practical style that required little maintenance.

Alex's wardrobe was a realm of muted colors and timeless styles, lined with jeans and khakis, and a row of casual button-downs and polo shirts. Navy blue and forest green were frequent choices, their earthy tones resonating with his grounded personality. His footwear of choice was a pair of well-worn gray sneakers, comfortable for his daily routine, as well as his long gaming sessions.

Sitting in front of his laptop, his fingers danced along the keyboard with speed and precision. As a data analyst, Alex spent his days sorting through spreadsheets, datasets, and numerous lines of programming code. It was a tedious existence, but a necessary means to sustain his true passion.

Often during his workday, Alex would gaze longingly at the video game memorabilia and posters scattered throughout his office. The virtual world was his portal to fantastical lands, his sanctuary from the mundane and the chaotic. It was how he honed his skills, forged bonds with like-minded gamers across the digital landscape, and discovered a sense of purpose that often eluded him in the real world. The city's bustling streets, with their cacophony of voices and constant demands, always seemed to fade away as he immersed himself in the digital reality of video games. There, he could work to conquer challenges, solve intricate puzzles, and solidify his virtual legacy.

In the world of PixelQuest, his preferred realm, Alex transformed into a legend known to all as Nexxus, a name that resonated throughout the PixelQuest universe. He was a legend who had achieved unparalleled feats in the realm of online gaming, and had a cache of rare loot to prove it. His journey from a novice player to a luminary and digital hero was nothing short of extraordinary, paralleled only by a player known as Xyra. She was a formidable gamer in her own right, though Alex had never had the opportunity to encounter her in his adventures.

But Nexxus' accomplishments extended beyond mere item

collection. He had conquered epic quests that challenged even the most seasoned adventurers. Whether it was slaying ancient dragons, solving intricate puzzles, or leading his guild to victory in intense guild wars, he approached each challenge with strategic brilliance and unwavering resolve. To Nexxus, the world of PixelQuest was not a mere game; it was a battlefield where his skills and tactics were put to the test.

Alex was proud of his achievements as Nexxus, but it paled in comparison to the community he had helped to build. He was a respected figure in the realms of PixelQuest, offering guidance and assistance to newer players and hosting events that brought the community together. His expertise and charisma made him a role model for aspiring gamers and an inspiration to many.

The real world, in contrast, was daunting and overwhelming to him, filled with unfamiliar conversations that seemed forced and awkward. He struggled to find common ground with others and often felt like an outsider in social situations. He yearned for the same level of ease and comfort in person as he experienced online, a desire that often felt like an unattainable dream.

As Alex logged out of his work for the day and prepared to escape into the virtual world, he noticed his cat, a fluffy and mischievous tabby named Whiskers, lounging lazily on the windowsill. Whiskers often provided a comforting presence amid the routine of his daily life, a source of solace and companionship in the solitary moments that were all too frequent.

Whiskers was a charismatic and independent feline companion who had been a part of his life for several years.

With his striking tabby fur and a set of charming, perfectly symmetrical white whiskers that earned his name, he was a constant source of comfort and occasional distraction in his otherwise ordinary world. His presence added a touch of warmth and unpredictability to the carefully structured life that Alex preserved.

Whiskers had a playful streak, often pouncing on shoelaces or chasing after a stray feather that drifted into the room. His antics provided moments of levity in the monotonous routine of Alex's daily life. When he was deep into work or lost in the virtual gaming world, Whiskers would curl up nearby, occasionally batting at the cords of his gaming headset or nuzzling his way onto Alex's lap to demand attention. His actions were the sole reminder that there was more to life than screens and pixels, a call to experience the tangible joys of the physical world.

Despite his playful nature, Whiskers also had a knack for sensing when Alex needed emotional support. Whenever Alex felt stressed or downcast, Whiskers would come to sit beside him, his soft purring and warm presence offering the companionship that Alex was sorely lacking in his life.

Alex smiled and walked over to the windowsill, where Whiskers stretched and pawed at the glass, trying to catch the fleeting rays of sunlight. He scratched the cat behind his ears, and Whiskers responded with a contented purr.

Alex laughed as Whiskers rolled onto his back and stretched languorously to his full length. It had become a daily routine after work, a clear indication that it was time for belly rubs.

"Three-thirty, on the dot. How do you always know?"

Whiskers let out a low meow, stretching again to indicate that his patience was wavering.

"Ok, I get it. Sorry." Alex said, stroking the soft fur of Whiskers' stomach.

Once Whiskers was satisfied with his daily ritual, Alex settled into his gaming chair and put on his headset. Whiskers sat at his feet, clearly unimpressed with the virtual worlds that often stole Alex's attention, but still content to support his companion. It was a simple gesture, but it filled Alex with a sense of comfort and reassurance, a reminder that he was not alone in his journey, both in the digital and physical realms.

The room was bathed in a soft, ambient glow, the radiant light from his computer screens casting enchanting shadows across the space. His gaming rig, a black behemoth that sat proudly on his desk, hummed with life, its cooling fans generating a symphony of white noise that lulled him into a sense of serenity. It was a calming background noise, signaling the beginning of another thrilling odyssey.

Alex's fingers danced lightly on the keyboard, and the soft click-clack of mechanical switches filled the room as he navigated through the game's intricate menu. With a sense of purpose, he selected his favorite character, the seasoned adventurer, Nexxus, ready to embark on yet another epic journey. The anticipation was palpable, a cocktail of excitement and eagerness coursing through his veins.

As the loading screen faded away, Alex found himself standing at the edge of a breathtaking virtual landscape. Verdant forests stretched as far as the eye could see, their towering trees swaying gently in an unseen breeze. Majestic mountains loomed on the horizon, their snow-capped peaks glistening in the warm light of the virtual sun. And in the distance, a mysterious dungeon entrance beckoned, promising hidden treasures and challenges waiting to be conquered.

For Alex, gaming was more than just a pastime; it was an escape, a chance to challenge himself, and a wellspring of endless entertainment. With his trusty headset snugly in place, he was prepared to lose himself in this meticulously crafted digital world, ready to tackle new quests, solve intricate puzzles, and forge alliances with fellow adventurers along the way.

The game's soundtrack, a symphony of orchestral melodies, enveloped him, transporting him deeper into the virtual realm. He closed his eyes for a moment, savoring the sensation of being fully immersed in the fantastical world before him. It was as if the borders of reality had blurred, and for this brief moment, he was truly a part of this mesmerizing universe.

As the music swelled, Alex opened his eyes, the shimmering landscape before him an invitation to begin his quest anew. There was a world to explore, challenges to conquer, and discoveries to be made. With a final deep breath, he set off, his steps echoing through the dense forest.

"Ouch!" A sudden, sharp pain shot through his foot, pulling him from his immersion. He looked down to find a small spot of blood on his toe, and a mischievous tabby cat, stretched lazily at his feet, looking up at him sheepishly.

Alex reached down to inspect his big toe, which had taken the brunt of the cat's unintentional attack. To his astonishment, an ethereal heads-up display materialized before his eyes, complete with a life bar, mana gauge, and an experience meter. The small scratch had caused a portion of his life bar to deplete, and he watched in disbelief as it slowly began to replenish with the subsiding pain.

He blinked, his mind reeling from the bizarre experience. "This can't be real," he muttered under his breath, attempting to rationalize the situation. He had heard tales of individuals experiencing vivid hallucinations under extreme stress or in heightened emotional states. Perhaps this was his mind's way of telling him to take a break from the virtual realm. That had to be it, he reasoned.

Despite his skepticism, Alex couldn't deny the palpable sensations and the persistent presence of the HUD. It felt so real, so tangible, that he found it difficult to dismiss as a mere hallucination. It was as if he had become a character in his own favorite video game, a notion that defied all logic.

As the initial shock began to wane, Alex took a moment to collect his thoughts and assess the situation. If this was indeed a hallucination, he needed to find a way to regain control of his thoughts and return to reality. He could only assume that this was a case of fatigue, or perhaps a vivid dream.

With these thoughts swirling in his mind, Alex reached for his smartphone, hoping to seek guidance from his gaming companions. His fingers brushed against the screen, but what he saw left him stunned. Instead of the familiar grid of app icons, an inventory display appeared, complete with slots for weapons, armor, and potions.

Alex stared at his phone in disbelief, tapping a few of the inventory slots. Icons representing everyday objects like his coffee mug and a pack of gum materialized, each with peculiar attributes and statistics. He even had an item labeled "Phone of Texting," which, according to its description, boosted his communication skills. "What the hell is wrong with me?" he mumbled, his voice tinged with incredulity.

Gazing around the room, Alex realized that the strange transformation wasn't confined to just his body and phone. Everyday objects had taken on a distinctly game-like appearance. His TV remote now featured buttons labeled "Fireball," "Jump," and "Pause." The gaming posters adorning his walls had transformed into interactive quest boards, each displaying glowing objectives to complete.

Alex rubbed at his eyes in a futile attempt to cast off the delusions he was experiencing. "Come on, Alex. Get it together."

Amid this surreal transformation, Whiskers leaped onto his lap and settled in, purring contentedly. Alex blinked in surprise as he noticed a speech bubble materialize above Whiskers' head. Inside it, a simple message blinked: "*Food, please.*"

"Holy... Whiskers?" Alex ventured, his gaze shifting to his feline companion. "Can you... can you understand me?"

Whiskers tilted his head, his eyes wide with a bewildered expression, and let out another "*Food, please.*"

A faint chuckle escaped Alex's lips at the absurdity of the situation. He was almost certain he was experiencing some sort of elaborate hallucination or lucid dream. So, what harm was there in playing along? He gently lifted Whiskers off his lap. "I don't know if I'm dreaming or losing my mind, but either way, I might need some sort of mental help." He shook his head before continuing, "Alright, buddy, let's get you some food." He headed to the kitchen, his thoughts a whirlwind of perplexity and amusement.

After filling Whiskers' bowl with kibble, he returned to his gaming chair, where his cat promptly resumed his position on his lap. Alex felt a strange sense of comfort having Whiskers by his side. In this increasingly surreal gaming experience, it was as if his cat was a grounding presence, a link to the real world that he desperately needed.

As he delved deeper into the digital landscape, battling virtual monsters and solving intricate puzzles, Alex couldn't shake the question that gnawed at him. How on earth was he going to make sense of this bizarre and fantastical experience? It was as if he had been transported into a video game, and there was no clear roadmap to navigate this uncharted territory.

But one thing was certain. Alex was in for a night of gaming unlike any other, with his loyal and mysteriously transformed cat, Whiskers, by his side, who seemed to be living out his own comical quest for "*Food, please.*"

As the night wore on, and Alex ventured deeper into the digital realm, he couldn't shake the feeling that something profound and extraordinary was unfolding around him. He was no longer a mere player; he had become a character in a living, breathing video game, and the rules of his reality had been rewritten. The lines between the digital and the tangible were blurring, and a grand adventure awaited, filled with mysteries, challenges, and the promise of discovery.

Two

Assemble the Tea Party

Waking up the next morning did little to ease his concerns. The buzzing of his alarm clock at the usual 7:00 AM was replaced with a digital melody akin to that of a quest update in the gaming world he was so fond of. He was, once again, greeted by Whiskers, the odd speech bubble returned with a far more demanding *"Food, now!"* replacing last night's more polite request. The grumbling in Alex's stomach seemed to echo the sentiment as he wiped the sleep from his eyes and stretched a bit before getting out of bed.

Alex's home appeared more game-like than it had the night before. Everywhere he looked, Alex was faced with strange digital artifacts and shimmering pixels. Out of habit, he checked his phone and found the inventory list blazing on the screen once again. "This is easily the most elaborate dream I've ever had," he said to himself as Whiskers nudged his elbow, as if pointedly drawing attention to his feline demand for breakfast. "Yes, Whiskers. I know the morning routine. You get food, then I get food." The satisfied purr in response indicated that, maybe, Whiskers understood more than he was letting on.

Up and dressed in his usual khakis and a pale lavender button-down shirt, Alex filled Whiskers' bowl before setting his sights on the coffee maker; the most important appliance in the house, given his lifestyle. He meticulously measured out the coffee grounds before filling the tank with water, then pressed the button and allowed the aroma of the freshly brewed, life-giving potion to overtake him. As he waited for the coffee to finish, he carefully sliced a bagel and placed both halves in the toaster before pushing down on the lever.

As he waited for his breakfast, he took a moment to look around the kitchen, taking in the strange glitches and artifacts digitizing his home. He thought back to the inventory screen on his phone, the small pixelated icons depicting the belongings he had on him. Pulling his phone out of his pocket, he said "If this dream has put me in a video game, I might as well test the game mechanics." He then scrolled down until he found the small icon resembling his coffee cup and, with a small sigh of resolve, gave it a tap.

He couldn't help but jump back a bit as the mug materialized in a digital flourish in front of him, even as it was exactly what he was expecting to happen. Hesitantly, Alex reached out to take the cup. As he wrapped his fingers around the digitized ceramic, the holographic surface became more solid, and the weight of it suddenly dropped into his hand. "So cool. Weird, but so freaking cool," he breathed excitedly.

Alex followed the intoxicating scent emanating from his unnecessarily complicated coffee maker as if lost in a desert and looking for water. As he poured his first cup, he allowed the warmth of the mug to soothe his still slightly trembling fingers. Coffee always calmed him, an effect he never fully understood given its nature as a stimulant.

Still, his first sip of coffee in the morning was always the official start to his day. The fragrant aroma, the boldness of the flavor as it first touched his lips, the gentle warmth flowing down through his chest. Every moment, every drop, was a gift of serenity and consciousness.

Today was no different. If anything, Alex's need was amplified by his slightly frayed nerves. His strange circumstances nagged at his mind, his dream-like surroundings seeming more and more real to him.

As Alex pulled away from his long, languid sip, he was once again startled by the glowing HUD appearing before him. He watched as the red health bar changed to vibrant, pulsing gold. Alex laughed nervously, slightly concerned by his lack of shock at this point. "Coffee must be a power-up in this world. First thing that's made sense about any of this," he quipped.

Some time later, Alex sat at his computer, the steady rhythm of keyboard clicks filling the silence. His half-eaten bagel sat on a plate in the corner of his desk next to his empty mug, his third cup of coffee being recently drained. It was then that the percussive melody of keystrokes was interrupted by a strange notification sound on his phone, a cheerful mix of notes that Alex had never heard before.

Alex, confused and a bit apprehensive, reached for the

device tentatively. As his fingers brushed the screen lightly, a glowing icon appeared in the shape of an envelope. "I guess that means I have mail?" he questioned to himself. Alex watched the small icon bobbing up and down on his screen for a moment longer, then he shrugged and gave it a quick tap.

Nothing happened. He tapped it again, then a third time. Still nothing. "Huh, I guess there are some limits to this world after all," he pondered. "Well, I needed a break anyway."

Alex slipped on his gray tennis shoes, chosen more for comfort than style. Tying his shoes proved more difficult than anticipated as a curious, slightly overfed tabby cat demanded his attention during the process.

"*You leave?*" the bubble appeared over Whiskers' head.

Alex, still somewhat unsettled by this new ability to communicate with his feline companion, responded, "Uh… yeah. I'm just going to the lobby to check the mail."

The speech bubble shimmered slightly, then changed. "*Come with?*"

Alex thought for a moment. "You know what? Sure, buddy. You can come. It's no stranger than anything else that's been happening."

Whiskers, seeming very happy with the situation, padded to the door and pawed at it lightly. "*See nice lady,*" he purred.

"Mrs. Jones?"

"*Outside. Can smell,*" another soft purr as the speech bubble changed again.

Alex knew it wasn't unusual to run into Mrs. Jones in the apartment building halls. He often suspected that she was lonely, given that he had never seen her with any visitors. In fact, Alex would often make a point to seek her out for that reason. "We both know she's a big fan of yours, too. Let's go say hi."

Alex had always known Mrs. Jones as a woman of a certain age, with soft silver hair that fell gracefully to her shoulders. Her hair was always meticulously styled, framing her face in loose waves that gave her an air of sophistication. She had a gentle, weathered face that hinted at a lifetime of experiences, and her warm brown eyes held a kind and welcoming gaze.

Her choice of clothing typically reflected her understated, refined taste. She favored pastel-colored cardigans, neatly pressed blouses, and knee-length skirts that flowed gracefully as she moved. Mrs. Jones was known for her pearl necklaces and simple gold stud earrings that added a touch of timeless elegance to her ensemble. Her shoes were sensible and comfortable, always chosen for practicality rather than fashion.

She had an aura of serenity about her, with a calm demeanor that made her approachable and easy to talk to. Mrs. Jones was the sweet, elderly neighbor who would exchange pleasantries in the lobby or offer him homemade cookies during the holidays. She was a pillar of normalcy in their quiet apartment building, always tending to her perfectly manicured roses in the community garden. But today, as he stepped out to collect his mail, something was different.

Mrs. Jones stood just outside Alex's door, her once-coiffed hair now slightly wild, with a wide grin on her face. Her clothing was disheveled and poorly matched, a far cry from the usual care and preparation she put into her appearance.

These things, however, were not the most shocking about Mrs. Jones appearance in the hall.

Alex couldn't believe his eyes. Mrs. Jones, his normally mild-mannered neighbor, stood in the dimly lit hallway of their apartment building, a quest marker glowing above her head like a non-player character in a video game.

"Mrs. Jones?" Alex ventured, feeling a strange mix of amusement and discomfort. "Are you... Is everything okay?"

Mrs. Jones turned to him, her eyes vacant, and a fixed smile on her face. Every movement and gesture was stiff and robotic, as if she was being controlled by an outside force. "Greetings, traveler," she said in a robotic tone. "I require your assistance."

Alex furrowed his brow. "Assistance with what, Mrs. Jones?"

Ignoring his question, Mrs. Jones produced a holographic map with the quest marker prominently displayed. "Your quest, should you choose to accept it, is to find the 'Teapot of Destiny.' It is of utmost importance."

Alex shook his head, unable to hide his bewilderment. He looked down at a slightly perturbed Whiskers, who remained ignored despite weaving between Mrs. Jones' legs for attention. *"Nice lady act strange."*

Alex gave Whiskers an empathetic glance before reaching down to give him a pat on the head, "I know buddy. I'm not sure what's going on either." He then directed his attention to the odd sight of the woman in front of him. "Teapot of Destiny? Mrs. Jones, what's going on here? Are you feeling alright?"

Mrs. Jones continued with her programmed responses,

completely detached from reality. "The Teapot of Destiny holds great power. The fate of our realm depends on it. Please, traveler, embark on this quest."

Alex scratched his head, feeling like he was caught in a bizarre and surreal video game glitch. "But why me? I'm not an adventurer."

Mrs. Jones remained unresponsive to his questions, her gaze fixed on the holographic map. "You have been chosen, traveler. The Teapot awaits. Good luck."

Alex reluctantly accepted the holographic map that was handed to him. "Mrs. Jones, what is going on around here? This whole thing is just too weird."

"You have been chosen, traveler." Mrs. Jones repeated. "The Teapot awaits. Good luck."

Alex shook his head, realizing that he had gotten all he was going to get out of Mrs. Jones. Though this had to be a dream, it was still way out of Alex's comfort zone. However, the excitement of the adventure that lay ahead was too alluring to resist. It was a dream come true, a chance to live out his PixelQuest adventures. Even if it wasn't real, at least he could enjoy it until he woke up.

With a final, quizzical look shared between Alex and Whiskers, he mumbled a quick goodbye to the unresponsive Mrs. Jones, and continued his descent into what surely had to be madness, or at the very least an abnormally vivid dream, his furry companion sauntering along behind him.

Three

Scripted Surreality

As Alex emerged from the entrance of the apartment building, he was confronted with a perplexing and surreal scene. The sky was mostly clear, save for a few strange polygons of cloud cover. The sun shone in dazzling rays, graphical anomalies floating in the light. The city, though familiar, had taken on a cartoonish, blocky visage, as if seen through a computer monitor.

The typically bustling sidewalk, which would usually have been filled with people walking their dogs, chatting with neighbors, or simply going about their daily routines, had transformed into an enigmatic spectacle. The surrounding people reminded him of NPCs from a virtual world, moving with a strange mechanical precision in repetitive patterns.

They walked along predefined paths, executing peculiar routines and parroting identical gestures and phrases like life-sized marionettes stuck in an endless loop. It was as if the very essence of their individuality had been subsumed into a scripted dance of conformity.

Alex squinted in disbelief, his senses assaulted by the uncanny spectacle before him. The morning sunlight bathed the scene in a surreal glow, casting elongated shadows that accentuated the bizarre nature of this reality. He cautiously approached one of the passersby, a middle-aged woman in a business suit who seemed locked in her peculiar role.

"Umm… excuse me," Alex called out, trying to engage her in conversation. "Excuse me?" he said louder, as the woman passed by without so much as a glance. Finally, he decided to step in her path, anxious to get answers about the unsettling scene.

The woman turned to him, her expression devoid of any warmth or spontaneity, her eyes glazed with an eerie vacancy. She responded with a voice that carried a disturbing, mechanical tone, "It's such a beautiful day," she said flatly. "I'm so glad I decided to walk to work."

"I'm… um… sorry to bother you, but…"

"It's such a beautiful day," she said again, sidestepping Alex and continuing down the sidewalk. "I'm so glad I decided to walk to work."

Alex blinked, taken aback by the robotic response. He decided to try again, thinking that perhaps the first encounter was an anomaly. Approaching another person, this time a man in a baseball cap, he asked with a hint of desperation, "Do you know why everyone is acting like this?"

The man, caught in the same inexplicable loop as the others, replied with a rehearsed monotony, "Beautiful weather we're having today. It's a great day to go to the park."

A shiver of unease coursed through Alex's spine as he realized that these people were not capable of engaging in normal conversations. It was as if they were trapped within a scripted narrative, unable to deviate from their designated roles.

He rubbed his eyes in disbelief, hoping that he would wake up from what must be a bewildering dream. But as he reached out and touched the nearby lamppost, feeling the rough texture under his fingertips, his sense of reality remained painfully intact. This was not just a dream; it was a bizarre and disconcerting reality that he could not escape.

He felt a sudden urge to run back to his apartment and lock himself inside as the boundaries between reality and the surreal blurred beyond recognition. But what would that solve? If this strange occurrence was real, it would take him soon enough. That much was clear. Perhaps the only way out was to finish the quest. Maybe then, he would find a way to fix this.

The urge to panic loomed on the horizon, but Alex clung to his last vestiges of rationality. As his surroundings began to pixelate and fragment, he couldn't help but be both awed and alarmed. The world he had known was unraveling before his very eyes, and he was powerless to stop it. Every object, every person, and every building seemed to be caught in the throes of a glitchy transformation.

Alex took a deep breath, attempting to quell the panic that threatened to consume him. He couldn't afford to lose his composure; he needed to find a way out of this madness. Glancing down, he found a reassuring presence at his side: Whiskers, his loyal feline friend, was by his side.

Whiskers had been a steadfast companion since Alex had

adopted the small kitten years ago. The bond they shared was unbreakable, and the cat had always been a source of solace and comfort. Though Whiskers had undergone his own transformation in this peculiar world, gaining the ability to communicate in mysterious ways, Alex was confident that the essence of his furry friend remained unchanged.

Despite the unsettling circumstances, Alex couldn't help but take solace in Whiskers' presence. The cat occasionally rubbed against his leg, purring softly as if to convey re-assurance. It was a comforting sensation, a reminder of the unbreakable bond they shared.

Alex and Whiskers crossed the eerily deserted street, devoid of the vehicles that usually traversed the pavement in droves. Passing by more of the robotic, NPC-like pedestrians on the opposite sidewalk, he felt the weight of the unknown pressing down on him. Whiskers trotted faithfully at his side, his tail flicking nervously as he observed their strange surroundings.

The park across from his building was usually a sea of tranquility, people often far too busy with their daily lives for such frivolity. This day, however, the dappled sunlight filtering through the leaves had an otherworldly quality, like a fantastical dreamscape brought to life.

But as they ventured deeper into the park, the peculiar nature of this world became increasingly apparent. The trees, once ordinary and familiar, now seemed to grow taller, their leaves taking on vibrant, lifelike hues. The transformation was undeniable, and the once-static NPCs, stuck in their repetitive routines, began to break free from their scripted behaviors.

Alex watched with a mixture of astonishment and trepidation as the NPCs started interacting with each other in ways that defied their previous monotony. It was as though some invisible force was breathing life into this digital realm, injecting it with an unexpected vitality.

Whiskers, too, seemed affected by the changes in their environment. He would occasionally bat at the leaves, his feline curiosity piqued by the newfound realism. He attempted to engage with the NPCs in his own unique way, whether through playful pouncing or gentle head-butts, only to be met with responses that were now more varied and organic.

Alex couldn't help but feel a glimmer of hope as he witnessed these transformations. Perhaps they were making progress in unraveling the mysteries of this strange world. He turned to Whiskers, the feline's eyes reflecting a curious mix of bewilderment and fascination.

"Do you see that, Whiskers?" Alex asked, his voice filled with cautious optimism. "It's getting worse. Hopefully we're getting closer to the truth."

Whiskers meowed in response, the enigmatic chat bubble above his head shimmering with the word "*See,*" as if acknowledging the subtle shifts in their surroundings.

As they continued their journey through the park, the verdant canopy of leaves overhead seemed to embrace them with a newfound vibrancy. The once-muted colors now danced with life, and the air was filled with the symphony of rustling leaves and distant bird songs.

Alex's thoughts raced, trying to piece together the bewildering puzzle that had become his existence. He couldn't shake the memory of a groundbreaking virtual reality technology he had read about, a technology so advanced that it promised to revolutionize the gaming industry. It was rumored to immerse players so deeply in the game world that they would experience it as if it were real.

Could it be possible that he had somehow become ensnared in this virtual reality game? And if so, how could he escape its confines and return to the world he knew? It was an insane concept; that he would become so immersed in PixelQuest that he would lose all sense of reality. But the alternative was that this was all real, and that was just impossible. These questions swirled in Alex's mind, a complex web of uncertainties that he was determined to untangle.

With each step he took, Alex felt a renewed sense of purpose and determination. Whiskers, his steadfast companion, was a silent source of strength, a reminder that they were not alone in this bewildering journey. Together, they pressed onward, ready to face whatever challenges lay ahead and uncover the truth behind this strange new world.

As they continued further into the transformed park, the situation escalated. The NPCs, once trapped in their repetitive routines, began to display unpredictable behavior. Some of them turned hostile, their faces contorted into eerie masks of anger, and they slowly advanced toward Alex and Whiskers with an unsettling determination.

"Stay close, Whiskers," Alex whispered urgently to his feline friend. He couldn't help but feel a rising sense of danger. These NPCs, once mere digital entities, now seemed capable of causing real harm.

With Whiskers at his side, Alex navigated a treacherous path through the increasingly chaotic park. He had to rely on his instincts and quick thinking to avoid confrontations with the unpredictable NPCs. At times, they would abruptly change direction or lash out with unexpected aggression, forcing Alex and Whiskers to retreat and find alternative routes.

The environment itself seemed to shift and contort with every step, as if responding to an unseen force. Trees would morph into bizarre shapes, their branches reaching out like skeletal fingers, and the ground would undulate beneath their feet, making each step a precarious endeavor.

Alex's sense of unease grew with each passing moment. He couldn't shake the feeling that they were being watched, that some malevolent presence was orchestrating this surreal nightmare. The conflict between his desire to uncover the truth and the growing danger of their surroundings weighed heavily on him.

Whiskers, too, was not immune to the escalating tension. His tail puffed up in alarm, and his whiskers twitched as he remained on high alert. The once-playful curiosity that had defined his actions had now given way to a vigilant wariness.

Amid the chaos and uncertainty, Alex's determination remained unshaken. He knew that he had to find a way out of this nightmarish reality and return to the world he knew. With Whiskers by his side, he pressed forward, ready to confront whatever challenges lay ahead, no matter how bizarre or perilous they might be.

Four

Co-op Quest

Alex and Whiskers had been wandering through the dense forest for what felt like an eternity. The foliage loomed above them, casting dappled shadows on the ground. The air was thick with an eerie silence, broken only by the occasional rustling of leaves or the distant call of an unseen bird. It was as if the forest itself held its breath, a foreboding harbinger of some unknown force.

Their journey had been fraught with confusion and uncertainty. The world around them seemed to shift and warp as if reality itself was confused by its strange circumstances. The trees, once towering and majestic, now appeared distorted, their branches twisting in unnatural ways. The ground beneath their feet felt solid one moment and ethereal the next, like walking on an earthen cloud.

Alex's mind was a whirlwind of questions and doubts. How had he ended up in this strange place? What had happened to the familiar world he knew? And what was the meaning of the Teapot of Destiny, the elusive treasure that had become the focal point of his quest?

As he trudged forward, his loyal companion, Whiskers, padded alongside him. The plump tabby had been a source of comfort in this bewildering world. His soft purrs and the gentle touch of his fur against Alex's leg were reminders of the real world, a world that seemed to be slipping away with every step they took.

Alex felt himself teetering on the brink of despair as he walked through an endless extent of tree-lined paths. He had nearly given up hope of making any progress when the forest finally opened into a clearing, sunlight breaking through the canopy to highlight a colossal, hollowed tree in its center. Its bark was ancient, etched with intricate symbols that pulsed with a faint, otherworldly light. The sight was mesmerizing, and Alex couldn't resist the urge to approach.

His fingers brushed against the rough surface of the tree's bark, and a shiver coursed through him. It was as if the tree itself held the secrets of this bizarre world, waiting to be uncovered. He could barely contain the relief he felt, finally finding a piece of the puzzle that might lead him to the Teapot of Destiny and out of this nightmare.

He traced the glowing designs on the tree bark with his finger, staring in awe at the unusual sight, but his reverie was abruptly interrupted by a soft, mocking voice from behind. "First time I've seen a literal tree-hugger."

Startled, Alex spun around to find a young woman standing there, a mischievous grin playing on her lips. She was dressed in a way that defied the natural aesthetics of the forest; a pair of well-worn jeans, a t-shirt from a band that was probably too trendy for him to recognize, and a sleek black leather jacket.

Her short, edgy hairstyle framed her face with a pixie-like charm, and her emerald green eyes sparkled with amusement. The woman before him exuded a confidence that caught Alex off guard. There was a force about her that Alex both admired and found himself wary of, though he couldn't explain why.

She continued to study him with that sly grin, her voice carrying a hint of sarcasm. "Is there something about this particular tree that's made you so... touchy-feely?"

Despite the intimidation he felt in her presence, Alex summoned the courage to respond. "Uh... yeah... I guess you could say that."

She chuckled, her tone tinged with sarcasm. "Sure, interesting. Well, I have shit to do. Say goodbye to your special tree friend." Alex continued to stare at her, blinking rapidly. After a moment, she let out an annoyed sigh and waved her hand dismissively. "Off you go. Time to sweep the grass or mow the sidewalk, or whatever other pointless, repetitive task you've been assigned."

Alex blinked again, utterly perplexed by her words. "What are you talking about?"

Her irritation only seemed to intensify. "You know, like the other mindless robots all over the city," she gestured wildly as if to emphasize her point. "I already have a quest, so I don't need yours. Just go about your day and let me go about mine."

Summoning a rare burst of confidence, Alex took a step forward, standing taller than before. "I'm not an NPC. I'm a player."

The strange woman's initial skepticism didn't wane. She crossed her arms, still watching him suspiciously. "This is a new tactic. Okay, if you're a player, prove it."

Alex fumbled for words, his anxiety creeping back in. "Well… I have a character sheet and an inventory… and I can move around and interact with objects."

She squinted at him, her skepticism deepening. "That doesn't prove anything. What's your name?"

Alex hesitated for a moment, not entirely comfortable revealing too much information. "It's…uh, Alex. My name is Alex."

Her raised eyebrow showed that this did little to assuage her suspicion. "Alex? That's it? You're not giving me much to work with here."

Feeling cornered, Alex countered, "What about you? What's your name?"

The woman's lips curled into a sly smile. "Fine, my name's Lucy."

Alex couldn't help but notice the intrigue in her emerald eyes as they locked onto his. There was a complexity to her, a layer of mystery that piqued his curiosity even further. It was as if she held a thousand untold stories behind that mischievous smile.

"And the quest you mentioned?" Alex pressed.

Lucy hesitated for a moment, then finally nodded. "Yeah, I have one. What's your point?"

"What is it?"

"You don't need to know that."

As if sensing his unease, Whiskers let out a soft meow and

nuzzled against Alex's leg, providing a small comfort in this bewildering encounter.

The awkward silence that followed was thick with suspicion and uncertainty. Both Alex and Lucy were hesitant to reveal too much about themselves, adding another layer to the already bewildering encounter.

Lucy finally broke the silence. "Well, this has been riveting, Alex, but I'm in a bit of a hurry, so…"

"Figures," Alex mused. "The first normal person I've met in this messed up world, and she has to be…"

"Be what, Alex the player?" Lucy interrupted. "A bitch? You can say it. I wear that badge proudly. I haven't met many people that are worth the effort of being nice, and so far you haven't disappointed."

Alex's face flushed in anger. "If you want to live your life pushing people away, that's your problem. But I have shit to do too, so do what you want, but I'm fucking over it."

Lucy stared at Alex for a moment, then a grin began to spread on her lips. "That's the first interesting thing you've said, Alex the player."

Bewildered, Alex gaped at the strange woman. "You were baiting me, weren't you?"

"Well, I had to be sure you were telling the truth, didn't I?" Lucy laughed as Alex furrowed his brow. "So, who's the fur ball?"

As if on cue, Whiskers gave a small meow before leaping into Alex's arms. With a small laugh as Whiskers nuzzled his cheek, Alex said "This is Whiskers. Until I met you, he's been the only normal one around here."

"Has he been doing the chat bubble thing? I'm still not quite used to that."

Alex gave a small shrug, "Okay, so... mostly normal."

Lucy grinned at the response, a more genuine smile than before. The expression made her emerald eyes sparkle in a way that caused Alex's breath to catch in his throat for a moment. Of course, it hadn't escaped his attention that she was pretty, but this side of her was far more interesting.

It took a moment for Alex to realize he had been staring. Looking away quickly, a light blush staining his cheeks, he said, "Well, it's quite a coincidence that we both stumbled upon this tree. Now I just need to figure out what it has to do with this 'Teapot of Destiny' stuff."

Lucy's eyes widened with a mixture of astonishment and suspicion. "You're after the Teapot too?"

Alex nodded, his confusion deepening. "Yeah, I mean, it's part of my quest, and hopefully my way out of this insanity. Are you looking for it too?"

Lucy hesitated for a moment, then finally nodded. "Yeah, I am. But I'm not sharing any information, if that's what you're after. Just because you're a player doesn't mean I can trust you."

Alex looked back to find Lucy on one knee giving Whiskers a light scratch under his chin, his favorite spot. Whiskers sat in front of her, purring contentedly, "*Like*" adorning the telltale bubble over his head. He gave his furry companion a quick nod before redirecting his attention to Lucy. "I learned a long time ago that his instincts are far better than mine when it comes to people. If he trusts you, I can work with that for now."

"Fair point," she replied as she raised her eyes to meet his. From her reaction, she didn't expect to see the bright smile that Alex gave her in that moment, and her own smile broadened in response. Perhaps this wasn't just a coincidence after all. "Okay, Alex. Maybe we can work together, for now. Let's see if we can figure out what this tree has to say."

Lucy, it seemed, was a puzzle in herself. Her green eyes held secrets, and her confident demeanor masked something deeper. She was not like the NPCs that populated this surreal world. There was an authenticity about her, a spark of individuality that set her apart.

Throughout their conversation, Alex couldn't shake his curiosity about Lucy. He had so many questions, but he knew better than to push too hard. Trust was a delicate thing in this bewildering world, and he didn't want to risk alienating his only potential ally.

"So, Lucy," Alex began cautiously, "how did you end up here?"

Lucy's grin faded slightly, and she looked away as if lost in thought. "It's a long story, probably pretty similar to yours, I assume."

Alex nodded, understanding the need for privacy in a world where trust was a rare commodity. "Fair enough. We all have our secrets, I suppose."

The surrounding forest seemed to hum with hidden mysteries, and the hollowed tree before them held the promise of answers. The Teapot of Destiny remained an enigma, and their quest was far from over. With each step they took, Alex couldn't help but feel that their paths had crossed for a reason, that their fates were intertwined in this strange world.

"So, have you found anything so far?" Lucy asked, bringing Alex back from his drifting thoughts.

"I'm… not sure. It feels like there's something just beneath the surface, something trying to escape, or communicate, or something."

"What about the symbols?"

Alex shook his head. "Not sure. It looks like a language of some kind, but none I've ever seen."

Lucy peered at the markings, shaking her head as well. "No, me neither. Very strange."

Alex placed his hand back on the hollow trunk. "It's warm, and there's a steady rhythm to it. Almost like… a heartbeat. Here, feel for yourself."

Lucy approached cautiously, reaching out slowly, her pearlescent purple nail polish sparkling in the golden rays of the sun. She looked at Alex, doubt still showing in her eyes. "You're sure about this?"

"I'm touching it, and nothing has happened to me," Alex retorted. "Just feel."

As Lucy's fingertips brushed against the rough bark, a flood of visions entered Alex's mind. He was soaring over a vast landscape, passing above forests and rivers, ruins of cities that seemed to have rotten from within. He watched as dozens of small farming villages passed, all showing signs of the same rot. His consciousness followed along a road, winding along the forest edge before branching off to the east. A distant, glowing city came into view over the horizon, vast and beautiful, before the vision ended abruptly and he was back in the clearing with Lucy and Whiskers.

"What the fuck was that?" Lucy demanded, jerking her hand away. "What did you do?"

"I... I didn't do anything," Alex mumbled, still in shock from the strange experience. "Maybe the tree was... I don't know... waiting for both of us?"

"You do know how insane that sounds, right?"

Alex laughed. "Have you looked around lately? What part of this isn't insane?"

Lucy looked at Alex for a moment, seeming perplexed by the whole endeavor. Finally, she said, "Fine, so let's say the tree wanted us both to see that. What the hell did it mean? And more importantly, what does it have to do with us?"

"I have no idea," Alex replied, his eyebrows furrowed in thought, "but did you see that city at the end of the road? Maybe that's where we'll finally get some answers."

Lucy shrugged. "It's as good a theory as any. If the tree needed both of us to activate it, there might be more puzzles coming that require two people. I guess that means we're stuck with each other for now."

Alex smiled. "Strength in numbers, right?"

As they stood in the clearing, the pulsing light of the tree's symbols gone dormant, they knew that the journey ahead would be filled with challenges, puzzles, and danger. But they also knew that they weren't alone in their quest anymore. Together with Whiskers, the loyal cat, they would unravel the mysteries of this world, uncover the truth behind the Teapot of Destiny, and find a way home.

Five

Goblins and Gambits

Navigating the pixelated forest proved to be difficult at times. The trees began growing larger and more densely packed, causing the path to narrow and, at times, disappear altogether. The thick canopy overhead made it nearly impossible to determine what direction they were traveling, and they soon lost the trail entirely at the edge of a small pond.

Lucy, arms folded, made no attempt to hide the scowl on her face. "Do you have any idea where we're going?"

Alex pulled the digital map he was given from his inventory and peered at it intently, finally giving up and throwing it to the ground. "Of course not! This map is useless. It tells us where to go, but not how to get there."

"I could help you with that." A trilled, sing-song voice startled them from behind. Whiskers let out a hiss of disapproval at the intruder that immediately caused Alex's stomach to lurch. "For a price, of course."

As the pair turned toward their unwelcome guest, Alex let out an audible gasp. "Are you... you're a..."

"Yes, yes, a goblin. The name is Rask, if you care to know. Now, back to business. Do you accept my offer?"

Lucy, seeming to have regained her senses far quicker than Alex, cocked an eyebrow at the strange little creature. "You haven't told us your price yet."

Rask considered for a moment before replying. "Oh, it's nothing you can't afford. Just... your souls." Lucy made a move as though she'd strangle the churlish little imp.

Rask held up his gnarled hands defensively. "Kidding, I'm kidding. So defensive. You humans just can't take a joke, can you? In truth, all I ask is that you solve a riddle. Should be easy for intelligent humans such as yourselves, right?"

Alex, finally recovering from the initial shock of being faced with a goblin, straightened a bit. "And if we don't?"

"Well, if you don't, or choose not to," a wide, toothy grin spread across the Rask's face, "I suppose you will have plenty of time to admire the scenery. Trust me, you'll be here a while without my help. I'm sure the hungry animals of this wood will appreciate your sacrifice, though."

Alex's stomach turned once again. "Okay, we get the picture."

Alex glanced at Lucy, who just shrugged in response. He then looked to Whiskers, who had taken a defensive stance with the hair on his back bristling. "*Don't like*" printed within the chat bubble atop his head.

Rask followed Alex's glance and laughed. "Your little beast

is an excellent judge of character, but it doesn't change the fact that I'm the only help you're going to get in these woods."

His shoulders dropped as he conceded. With a sigh, he said, "Alright, out with it then. Hit us with the riddle." Alex glanced at Lucy, his eyes filled with determination. "We've got this," he whispered to Lucy.

Rask clapped his hands, squealing with delight. "Wonderful, wonderful! A game it is, then." He stopped suddenly, placing a single twisted index finger against his pursed lips. "I must think a moment. This riddle must be tailored to the stakes at hand." He extended his finger toward the two adventurers, the jagged nail caked with grime, and gave it a shake, as if scolding them. "I can't go easy on you. I do hope you understand." With another giggle, he began pacing, deep in thought.

Moments later, the silence of the glade was broken yet again by the shrill, squealing laughter of the little goblin. "Oh, I've got it. I've got it!" Rask turned sharply toward Alex and Lucy, his eyes dancing with excitement. "Now listen closely, because I'm only going to say this once, and you only get one chance at this. My riddle will lead you to a hidden treasure within this forest glade. Bring it to me, and you shall have my assistance."

Lucy, visibly annoyed with the goblin, gave a curt nod. "Agreed."

"Very well then, here we go." Rask rubbed his hands together as if preparing for a meal.

"Within nature's cradle, where whispers softly sing,

A hidden treasure sleeps, like a phoenix's final wing.

In the heart of tranquility, where life's flames find rest,

Discover this enigma, in life's gentle caress.
Amidst the guardians of green, where secrets reside,
it awaits your keen eye, earth and sky coincide.
In this serene haven, where mysteries lay,
Find the fire in water, as night turns to day."

"And exactly how long do we have to figure this out? Is there a time limit?" Alex asked, mulling the lines over and over in his head.

Again, Rask's crooked finger came up in the scolding motion he seemed so fond of. "It seems that someone wasn't paying attention. No hints, no repeating. Figure it out, and my assistance is yours."

"Oh, come on!" Lucy exclaimed, growing more and more annoyed by the moment. "You won't even give us a time frame?"

The dingy goblin considered for a moment, then shrugged. "Okay, fine. I'm feeling generous today, so I'll give you one hint, but only one. You two may want to find a comfortable spot to settle in. You'll need your rest before this is done."

Lucy was pacing as she thought, then stopped mid-stride. "Shit," she said softly, but with feeling. She turned to Alex with a defeated look on her face. "He's right. We need a place to sleep for the night."

Alex looked back at her quizzically. "Why? What have you figured out?"

"'...As night turns to day'. We can't solve this until sunrise. We're stuck here for at least twelve hours."

"Oh, you are a smart one, aren't you? For a human, at least."

Alex went from confused to annoyed, and finally to angry.

He wheeled on Rask, only to find that the goblin had vanished. He yelled into the clearing, assuming Rask must still be within earshot, "We have to get the hell out of here now! What kind of crap are you pulling? Why are you keeping us here?"

"We made a deal. You agreed to my game." The shrill tone from behind Alex made him jump once again. Rask sat on a nearby rock, inspecting his dirty fingernails as if bored with the conversation. "We never discussed terms. If there was to be a time limit, you probably should have mentioned that beforehand."

The anger that had welled up in Alex deflated. He had been so distracted by the mere presence of a goblin that it never occurred to him to negotiate. This was no more Rask's fault than his own.

"Now, if you'll excuse me, I have other matters to attend to. But don't worry, I'll know when I'm needed here." The goblin allowed himself a wide grin that nearly swallowed his narrow face, revealing pointed, needle-like teeth. "See you soon, friends." With a small wave and a flash of light, he was gone.

After staring a bit longer at the rock where Rask had perched only moments ago, Alex turned to Lucy with a sigh. "So, what now?"

Lucy looked around the grove, overlooking the clear water of the pond at its center. "Well, there's not much we can do tonight except try to find some shelter and get comfortable."

"Any chance you have a tent in your inventory?" Alex asked sardonically.

"Sorry, the best I have is a bedroll I picked up in the city. Just one though. Never thought I'd need more than that."

Alex gave a wry smile that didn't quite reach his eyes. "No worries. The ground looks soft by the pond."

"Don't be stupid, Alex." Lucy's soft tone drew Alex's eyes to her own. "We're both adults here. We can share the bedroll." As Alex began to protest, Lucy took a step closer. Placing a hand on his arm, her green eyes glistened with sincerity as she said, "It will be fine. I'm not going to make you sleep on the ground. I'm not that much of a bitch." The corner of her mouth twitched into a slight grin.

Alex felt her touch as though she were pure electricity, every volt traveling from her fingertips, up his arm, and to his very soul. His heart sped up and his mouth grew dry. He had never had this feeling before. He certainly never felt like this in his virtual encounters, and his limited physical interactions paled in comparison to this one simple touch. It took him a moment to realize that Lucy was waiting for a response, but all he could manage was a nod.

Lucy's hand dropped away as she stepped back to start preparing for the night, but the electricity stayed a while longer. As his pulse finally slowed, logic began to reenter his mind. It was just a reassuring touch. She was just being nice. Of course, she trusted him. She had probably figured out that he was too boring to be a threat. She probably pitied him more than anything else. How stupid of him to think for one second that it could be more.

He forced a smile as he attempted to cover his perceived stupidity with humor. "You just want to make sure I don't slow you down tomorrow with a sore back, don't you?"

Lucy glanced back at him with a mischievous grin that would have made Rask proud. "Now you're catching on, Alex. Glad we're on the same page."

Alex's smile grew more genuine at the reply. When she looked at him like that, he just couldn't help it.

It took some time to prepare for their evening's rest. They each searched their inventories for useful items, which seemed to be few and far between, then collected firewood and water from the forest and pond around them. Eventually, they found themselves sitting on a felled log under the starry pixelated skies, warming by a crackling digital campfire. Whiskers had found a patch of soft grass to curl up near the fire, seeming just as comfortable here as he would have been in his little bed at home.

The two sat in near silence until the moon was high overhead. The conversation had been limited, as if anything further would make them too vulnerable to each other. Alex cleared his throat, breaking the awkward silence that had settled between them. "Well, it looks like we're in for an interesting night, huh?"

Lucy chuckled nervously, her cheeks tinged with a soft blush. "Yeah, it seems that way."

They spread the bedroll on the forest floor, their proximity causing a new level of tension to bloom. As they settled in, they realized there wasn't much space to spare. They lay there side by side, barely an inch between them, their bodies awkwardly angled to fit on the narrow bedroll.

Lucy turned slightly, trying to get more comfortable, and her fingers brushed against Alex's arm. She jerked her hand away, stumbling through an awkward apology. "Sorry, I...

this isn't exactly... you know... what I had in mind when I left my apartment this morning."

Alex turned toward her, his eyes locking onto hers. "No need to apologize. Sometimes life takes us on unexpected journeys."

Their faces were mere inches apart now, the tension in the air palpable. Alex's breath seemed to sync with Lucy's, their heartbeats creating an unspoken rhythm that spoke volumes.

As the night deepened, they found themselves exchanging whispered stories and dreams, sharing their innermost thoughts beneath the forest canopy. The awkwardness gave way to a growing connection, their laughter breaking through the initial discomfort.

"Remember that mushroom along the path you thought was a treasure chest?" Lucy teased.

"I swear, it looked like one! I've never seen a mushroom that big." Alex chuckled, shaking his head. "I won't live that down, will I?"

Their playful banter and shared laughter filled the forest with a warmth that defied the chilly night air. It was as if the craziness of the world around them faded away, leaving the two of them in their own cozy, quirky bubble.

As the night wore on, they both realized that despite the awkwardness of their situation, there was something undeniably comforting about sharing that narrow bedroll. The physical closeness seemed to reflect the emotional connection that had been growing between them since they first met. As sleep finally began to claim them, their hands brushed against each other, their fingers intertwining naturally, as if they were meant to fit together.

***

Alex woke just before dawn to a distinctive avian chorus from the trees above. Countless bird songs echoed in the waxing light, more than he'd ever heard before. He was beginning to understand why people enjoyed camping, getting lost in the natural beauty of this place. Whiskers was already awake and very interested in the cacophony of bird songs as well, though likely for a very different reason.

As Alex stood within the shadows of the massive tree line, his thoughts drifted to the riddle they were given. He began reciting it softly to himself, hoping for some inspiration to leap out at him. "Within nature's cradle, where whispers softly sing, a hidden treasure sleeps, like..." A sudden thought occurred to him. "Lucy! Lucy, wake up!" He nearly ran to her in his excitement.

Lucy stirred slightly, then stretched as one eye opened, then the other. "Okay, okay, I'm awake. What do you want?"

Alex smiled sheepishly. "Sorry to wake you, but I think I have something."

Lucy sat up abruptly at this. "The riddle? You found the treasure?"

"Well, not quite," Alex said shyly, "but I think I have a couple of these clues figured out."

Lucy rubbed at her eyes and stretched. "Let's get to it then, Einstein." Lucy flashed her signature sly grin that nearly made Alex forget what he had to tell her.

Alex felt the heat in his cheeks once again and turned away to hide the telltale blush that would come with it.

"Yeah, um… So, the beginning... 'Within nature's cradle,'" he gestured to the surrounding grove, "'where whispers softly sing,'" he pointed up at the branches of the tree canopy above them.

Lucy looked perplexed for a moment before realization dawned on her. "The birds! Of course!"

Alex, still looking excitedly toward the treetops, mused, "So we'll find the treasure while the birds are singing, right?"

"I'm with you so far. Anything else?"

Alex met her gaze. "Yeah, the second part. 'A hidden treasure sleeps, like a phoenix's final wing.' When a phoenix dies, it burns to ash, right? Then it's reborn and rises from the ashes. Whatever we're looking for needs to rise from somewhere, so it's probably buried somewhere."

Lucy seemed to consider for a moment. "No, not buried. It's in the water. 'In the heart of tranquility,'. Water is the element of tranquility. It has to be in the pond."

Alex was nodding along in encouragement. "Okay, makes sense... But where in the pond? We don't even know what we're looking for. How are we going to find it in there?" He gestured desperately toward the shallow pool. "And what about the second half? Obviously, it starts out talking about the trees and the grove, but the part about finding fire in water? I don't know much about this world, but I can nearly guarantee you there's no fire in that pond."

Lucy stood from her seated position on the bedroll, wiping the sleep from her eyes as she did. "It has to be a metaphor. Something that..." Her words stopped abruptly as she noticed that the sun had crested the tree line, casting a single ray of golden light through the canopy, directly to the center of the pond.

Alex followed her gaze, slightly confused, until a red glint of reflected light caught his eye from below the water's surface. "Is that...?"

Lucy grinned wildly at the sight. "A ruby! I've heard it called a fire stone before. Fire in the water."

Alex's grin widened as well. "We found it!"

"Well, we spotted it," Lucy retorted, "but now someone has to go get it."

"You spotted it," Alex offered in return, "so I'll go get it."

Lucy's eyes widened in mock surprise as she fanned herself with her outstretched fingers. In a thick, faked southern drawl she exclaimed, "My, my, such a gentleman. What a lovely surprise."

"Quiet, before I decide to throw you in there after it," Alex quipped, a small smile tugging at the corners of his mouth to spite his feigned annoyance. Removing his shoes and socks, Alex then began to wade into the clear, shallow water.

Lucy's laugh echoed throughout the clearing, accompanied by the sound of splashing water and the birds above, as Alex went to retrieve their prize.

Six

Whispering Wood

"You little shit! We had a deal!" Lucy was furious. "We found your damn ruby. Now it's your turn to pay up."

Rask lounged on a nearby rock, inspecting his new treasure gleefully. The red of the ruby reflected on his pale green skin to cast a sickly brown glow across his face. " I believe the bargain was that I would help you if you were successful, and help you, I shall. I did not, however, promise to guide you."

Alex, mirroring Lucy's irritation at the double-talking goblin, took a step forward. "And how, exactly, do you intend to help then?"

Rask, still fixated on the ruby he held between his spindly fingers, waved his free hand as if swatting at an annoying insect. "Oh, it's quite simple, really. Just head east, between those two rocks over there." Another half-hearted wave of his hand gestured loosely to their left. "Less than a mile in, you'll crest a ridge, and a path will be on the other side."

Alex took a deep breath and calmed a bit. "So that's it? Less than a mile north, and we find the path we're looking for?"

The infuriating goblin tore his eyes from the gem long enough to flash a devilish grin at Alex. "I said a path. I didn't say the path. I only promised to help you get out of the woods. Your destination is entirely up to you."

Alex, normally calm and collected, felt his face redden with fury. He picked up the nearest rock and threw it at Rask, just to watch as it clattered harmlessly against the suddenly vacant stone seat.

"I would offer to amend the terms, of course, but the cost would be far greater than just a shiny rock. More than you would wish to pay, I think." Rask continued, now just out of Lucy's reach by the water's edge.

Lucy glared at the goblin with such intensity that Alex almost pitied the pathetic creature. Her words were short and clipped, and dripped with venom. "I think we've had enough of your help. Get out of my sight, you gangrenous little demon."

Rask's grin only widened further. "Well, I see that you two have places to be, as do I. Farewell friends." He gave a condescending little wave, then he was gone.

"Son of a..." Alex let out a long sigh, his shoulders visibly settling as his anger abated. "Well, at least we have a direction. It's better than what we had yesterday, I guess."

"True," agreed Lucy, "but I still wish I could get my hands around that damn goblin's throat."

"Trust me," replied Alex, "if I ever see that arrogant little ass again, it will be far too soon."

Quickly recovering their items from their makeshift

campsite, Alex and Lucy set their sights toward the east. Pushing through the thick underbrush, they were quickly swallowed by the forest once again.

Though the forest was thick and overgrown, the minuscule rays of sunlight that managed to pierce the canopy were enough to keep them on an eastward course. It was a slow trek, made more perilous than expected by the gnarled tree roots protruding from the ground, as if consciously attempting to impede their progress. Everything about this forest seemed intent on keeping them from moving forward. Alex had the sense that there was always movement in his periphery, but every time he turned to look, all would be still.

"Alex, stop!"

Alex hadn't heard that tone in Lucy's voice before. It was enough to overtake him with a chill of panic. He turned to find Lucy looking around, searching the woods frantically. Instinctively, he lowered his voice to a near whisper. "What's wrong?"

Lowering her voice in response, Lucy kept searching as she replied. "Do you hear that?"

"I don't hear anything. What is it?" Alex began scanning the environment as well.

"Exactly! I hear nothing. No wind rustling the trees, no wildlife. What happened to the birds in the clearing?"

The chill Alex felt matured to full-on dread at the thought. "Have you been seeing the movement, too?"

"I thought I was just being paranoid. Are we being hunted?" Lucy dropped to a crouch, as though she could disappear altogether if she made herself small enough.

"I think it's much, much worse than that." Alex's mind was

racing, trying to consider the best course of action. "Listen to me. I need you to come to me. Stay calm, just come here. I need you to take my hand. And no matter what happens next, do not let go."

Lucy looked too terrified to argue. She slowly raised herself back up to standing, then inched her way to Alex's side. As her hand slid into his, he could feel the trembling in her fingers, and he hoped that she didn't notice the same in his. "Okay, what now?" she whispered.

He looked into her sparkling green eyes, hoping it would not be the last time he did so, and gave a quick nod. He waited a moment for a nod back, confirmation that she was ready for whatever he had planned, before mouthing a single word to her. "Run!"

Together, they fled through the mass of tree trunks and limbs, hand in hand, hoping that the petulant goblin had been true to his word and had not just sent them here to die. The two moved in unison, weaving through the trees as they twisted and writhed, sentient beings trying to keep them prisoner. Whiskers followed close behind, darting around obstacles with speed and agility, intent on seeing his friends through this nightmare.

A small group of oaks closed ranks in front of the trio before they could slip through, but Alex deftly changed direction without slowing, pulling Lucy behind him. Another tree swung a low-hanging branch that caught Alex square in the temple, a gash immediately flowing bright red with blood. Alex was dazed by the impact and stumbled, but he managed to keep his footing. His legs burned, his chest ached, and still, he kept running.

"There Alex! Right there!"

Alex spared a quick glance at what Lucy was pointing at. It was an opening in the tree line leading to a small ridge and, presumably, the promised path beyond. Alex didn't hesitate. He dodged past a bushy maple as it moved to block his path, then ducked beneath the outstretched branch of a gnarled oak. Lucy matched him, stride for stride, as Whiskers picked his way through the chaos with little effort.

Alex finally felt a small amount of relief as they reached the opening. He pulled Lucy in closer to him before leading her out first, stealing one last glance behind at the forest that tried to swallow them whole.

Unfortunately, that stolen moment proved costly, as a root lifted from the soil and wrapped around Alex's ankle. He felt the tug before he realized what had happened. The relief he had felt only moments ago was washed away in a flood of pure panic. Lucy, feeling a tug of resistance that hadn't been there previously, instinctively wrapped her free hand around Alex's wrist and began to pull back, fighting against the strength of a sentient forest.

Alex began kicking and clawing at the ground, making every possible attempt to gain leverage so he could pull away from the grasping root, but there was nothing he could do. He was caught in a tug-of-war, and he knew who was going to win. He looked at Lucy, fighting frantically to pull him free, and a sudden resolve flooded through him.

"Let go." He said quietly.

"What?!" Lucy's shock was evident, but she kept pulling, her heels digging into the ground.

"Let go Lucy." His voice was quiet but steady, a surprise even to him. "I can't let you be taken too. Just let go."

Her eyes locked on his with fierce determination as she simply said, through gritted teeth, "No."

"Lucy, just let me..."

"No!" Lucy's voice was full of anger, but her eyes were full of tears. "I cannot lose another... I will not lose you, to a goddamn pile of firewood." She broke eye contact then, as if afraid of what Alex might see in that moment.

Alex never got a chance to continue the argument, as an approaching commotion caught his attention. An arrow, engulfed in blue flame, sailed over their heads and lodged in the base of the nearest tree. The surrounding foliage recoiled, seemingly in pain, as the root holding Alex loosened. The sudden release allowed Lucy to pull Alex to safety, as more arrows began to fly. The edge of the forest began to recede, retreating from the onslaught of those who approached.

Alex felt a strong pair of hands reach down to help him to his feet, and another hand was offered to Lucy for the same purpose. As Alex regained his composure, he turned to address his rescuers. However, the sight before him had him fumbling for words. A glance at Lucy proved that she, too, was at a loss.

The three beings standing before them were captivating, with a surreal and ethereal quality that made them seem like living works of art. Their features were humanoid and graceful, and they moved with an elegance that mirrored the world around them. Their pale, blue skin was slightly pixelated and emitted a subtle glow that Alex couldn't help but compare to an old video game character.

"It is fortunate that we were patrolling this stretch of the treeline." The closest of the three took a cautious step forward, seeming to have picked up on the newcomers' apprehension after such an ordeal.

Based on the embellishment of his uniform, Alex assumed this to be the leader of the group. The clear hierarchy focused his thoughts, allowing him to regain his voice. "Nobody here is more appreciative than I am, trust me. Thank you for helping us."

The radiant stranger put a fist to his chest and gave a small bow. It was an oddly formal gesture for such a chaotic world. "It was our pleasure, traveler."

"And what is your pleasure going to cost us?" Lucy eyed the strangers nervously as she spoke. She seemed rattled, tired, and not the same as the woman he had spent the night with.

"Ah, that explains how you've found yourself here. You've met Rask, I take it?"

"Yes, we've had the displeasure," Lucy said with a sour face.

"Well," the stranger's face mirrored hers at the thought, "that harmonically hindered musemisfit..."

"Captain!" The clear admonishment came from the woman standing by his side.

"Right, pardon my language... that goblin takes great pleasure in always telling the truth, but never the whole truth. Regardless, you are wise to be cautious of strangers in this land, but I assure you that you owe us nothing for our assistance. It is our duty to keep these lands safe for all."

"And what lands might those be?" Lucy asked

He stiffened suddenly, as if struck. "Mother of the Muse,

where are my manners? Welcome to Luterre. I am Helios Pixelhart, Captain of the Lumoran Guard. This," he gestured to the man on his left, "is Phelan, a newcomer to the guard but, I think you would agree, an excellent archer. And this is..."

The woman to his right stepped forward, her hand outstretched to Lucy. "Lieutenant Aurora Artisynth. Second in command and, " Aurora flashed an annoyed look at her captain, "perfectly capable of making her own introductions."

Lucy grinned as she took the outstretched hand, sparing a glance at the Captain, who seemed rather embarrassed to have committed such a sizeable overstep. "Oh, I think I'm going to like you, Aurora. Lucy Watts. Nice to meet you."

Aurora returned the grin before offering her hand to Alex. "And you are?"

"Alex. Alex Porter. Nice to meet you. And this is... Whiskers?" Alex looked around to find that Whiskers was gone. He looked around frantically, finally catching sight of his furry companion weaving around Phelan's legs, purring contentedly.

Phelan shrugged sheepishly. "I'm a cat person."

Whiskers meowed happily back at Alex, *"Smell like good!"*

Alex shook his head and laughed. "I guess we don't have to ask for Whiskers' opinion, do we?"

Captain Pixelhart cleared his throat, drawing everyone's attention. "Alex... Lucy..." he paused as he gave a nod to each, "my apologies for cutting this short, but this is truly not the best place for introductions. The trees are not the only things lurking at the forest's edge. Perhaps we should guide you to

Lumora. I trust you could use a night of food and rest after everything you've endured."

"If you wish it, of course," Aurora interjected. "The Captain seems to forget that you have no reason to trust us yet, and may take his rather formal invitation as more of an order."

The Captain, again embarrassed by his misstep, began blustering, "Yes, yes, of course. Apologies. I am not so good at interactions with others. You are, in no way, obligated to come with us. The offer is available to you, however, if you choose to accept."

Alex chuckled a bit as he watched Helios' face flush, a lavender that nearly matched his shirt. "Captain, I know the feeling." He looked to Lucy, a silent question in his eyes. Lucy nodded back, seeming far more relaxed with the encounter than she was at first. "We would be honored to join you and see your city."

The group began their journey towards Lumora, with their new companions leading the way. Alex and Lucy couldn't help but marvel at the beauty of the forest around them. The trees were tall and majestic, and the ground was covered in a layer of soft moss that seemed to glow in the dim light. It was hard to believe that such a peaceful place could be so dangerous.

As they walked, Helios explained more about Lumora and its people. The city had been built on top of an ancient ruin, and its inhabitants had learned to harness the power of magic to protect themselves from the dangers of this world. He spoke with pride of the history of the city as an artisan's utopia, an epicenter of culture and vibrancy. He also spoke about his own experiences as a member of the Lumoran Guard, and how he had dedicated his life to protecting those who couldn't protect themselves.

Alex, meanwhile, kept a watchful eye on their surroundings. He knew that they were still in danger, despite the company of guards in their midst. He couldn't shake off the feeling that something was watching them from within the shadows of the forest.

Beyond the lush foliage, the city of Lumora slowly emerged, appearing like a mirage through the trees. An aura of colored light emanated from the city like a small aurora, blues and greens reaching to the clouds and beyond. It was a city of breathtaking beauty, its buildings rising gracefully into the sky, architectural wonders adorned with intricate murals and vibrant mosaics. Each structure seemed to be a masterpiece in its own right, as if the entire city was an ever-evolving canvas.

"It's just like the vision," Alex said, wide eyed with disbelief.

"What vision would that be?" Helios asked.

"There was this tree in a clearing with glowing marks…"

"Ahh, I see," Helios interrupted. "You found the Sapiarbus. The Tree of Wisdom. I'm impressed, Alex. He doesn't speak to just anyone. You must be very special, indeed."

"It didn't talk to me alone," Alex corrected. "Lucy and I could only see the vision when we touched it together."

"Wait!" Helios stopped, turning slowly to take a better look at the newcomers. "Both of you? Together? That could only mean…" A smile spread across his face as his words trailed off.

"What are we missing?" Lucy asked, suspicion flaring in her eyes.

"Come! We need to get to the palace."

Their steps quickened as they drew nearer, a sudden need for haste apparent, but not entirely understood. The gentle rustling of leaves became a harmonious chorus, like a symphony of whispers from the enchanted forest. Alex felt his tension slowly ease at the change in atmosphere, no longer feeling the dread of unseen threats. It was as if the very trees were singing a welcome song, a melody that resonated with a sense of wonder and awe, and above all, comfort. Bird-like creatures with bright, luminous plumage soared through the air, their wings creating a melodic hum as they glided gracefully overhead.

The sight of Lumora and the enchanting sounds that surrounded them left Alex and Lucy spellbound, overshadowing the confusion of moments ago. They could feel the magic of this city coursing through their veins, and the promise of adventure and discovery hung in the air like an intoxicating perfume. As they stepped toward the city's gates, they knew that their journey had taken an extraordinary turn, and Lumora held secrets and wonders that would forever change them.

"This... this is..." Alex couldn't find a word strong enough to describe what he was seeing.

Lucy, eyes wide with awe, finished for him. "...spectacular."

Aurora turned to the pair, beaming with pride. "Welcome to Lumora."

Seven

Light's Crescendo

The gates adorning the entryway to Lumora were hardly gates at all, but elegant archways secured by a finely crafted iron portcullis, the bars gleaming as if polished daily. The stones were smooth as riverbed rocks and beautifully carved with runes that Alex assumed were from an ancient language of these people. Much like the Sapiarbus, a dim blue glow emanated from each carving, leading Alex to believe that these runes were the secret to harnessing the power of this land.

Two guards stood at the top of the wall watching vigilantly for any signs of trouble. Two more stood just inside the portcullis, also keenly aware of every movement outside their walls. All four put fists to their chests as the Captain approached and gave a deep, elegant bow, a gesture similar to the one Helios made during his introduction. Still, Alex found it oddly grandiose for a guard, even to his or her captain.

"Why so formal?" Lucy asked Helios, apparently mirroring Alex's thoughts.

"Because he is..." Aurora was quickly silenced by a terse look from her commanding officer. "He is an important man in this city. He is due the respect that affords him."

Lucy looked like she wanted to question the odd inter-action, but chose to remain silent. Instead, she looked to Alex with a quizzical shrug, a silent suggestion to address the strange behavior at a later time. Alex nodded in agreement, knowing that trust would need to be established on both sides before either would feel comfortable revealing their secrets.

The portcullis raised soundlessly to allow the small group entry, an engineering marvel in itself given the size and weight of such a construct. As they passed, the two guards within flanked the group, apparently cautious of outsiders. Alex could hardly blame them, in a land such as this, though he did spare a glance back nervously to see just how closely they were being guarded.

To his surprise, he found one of the guards smiling at him. The guard to his left, a younger man similar to him in height, spoke first. "You look nervous. Don't be. If Helios thought you might be a threat, you'd never have made it to our gates. All this..." He made a circular motion with his gloved hand, "is mainly for appearances. Need the people to know they're safe in the city. I'm Zephyr, by the way."

"Alex. Nice to meet you. And you are?" Alex's eyes shifted to the older man on his right.

"Name's Auril." He said in a gruff tone. "Zeph's right. If you were a threat, Helios woulda' left you where he found you, or worse. Still, you're outsiders, and we can never be too careful 'bout outsiders."

Alex nodded slowly. "No, I don't suppose you can." Alex

looked around a bit before glancing back at Auril. To protect a city like this, he would probably feel the same way.

Entering Lumora was like exploring DaVinci's canvas. Everywhere Alex looked within the city, there was a new piece of art to admire. The streets were paved in masterfully cut mosaic tiles. The lampposts were ornate pillars of carved stone topped with hammered bronze braziers lit by pale blue flame that danced in such a graceful manner that it could never be confused for typical firelight. Each building, each home and shop, was meticulously designed to mitigate the perfect blend of form and function. It was very clear that the Lumorans were nothing short of master craftspeople, and Alex found himself longing to see every inch of the city.

As they walked through the central road of Lumora, dozens of curious citizens gathered. All seemed to bow as Helios Pixelhart walked past, a gesture that Alex was beginning to suspect held more meaning than the Captain was letting on. As Alex and Lucy passed, many were simply content to satiate their curiosity, while several others murmured tentative greetings to the newcomers. It wasn't necessarily the warmest of greetings, but it certainly wasn't hostile either. It seemed these people had as much faith in the Captain as the rest of the guard did.

Continuing through the streets, the artistic history of Lumora became more and more apparent. Pixel-art murals adorned many of the older buildings, while the newer structures were decorated with more geometric, brightly colored pieces. Finally, as they approached the heart of the city, they began passing buildings and homes built with flowing lines and more contemporary flares not found in the more simple structures seen previously, displaying similar canvases of the brightest and most variegated hues. These recent murals had moved away from the baroque and expressionist tones of the earlier works, taking on a variety of new styles from abstract to impressionist, surreal to hyper-realism.

The city was breathtaking in a way that Alex could never imagine seeing in the real world. He glanced at Lucy to gauge her reaction, and found her transfixed on something directly ahead of them, mouth agape in astonishment. Following her gaze, Alex Found himself mirroring her absolute awe.

Towering above, several spires of glistening white marble had entered their view, as if growing from the horizon itself. Golden embellishments glistened from the pointed tops and flared eaves of each roof, and banners of rich, vibrant red hung down along the polished surface, embroidered with metallic yellow thread. As they drew closer, Alex realized that it wasn't metallic thread, but actual gold, somehow spun into embroidering floss to create a magnificent standard. The masterful tapestries, depicting the visage of a lion wielding a paintbrush as a weapon, caught and reflected the brilliant sunlight like a beacon. Alex saw it for what it was; a message to the rest of the world that these people would fight to defend the beauty of this city and its people.

"Beautiful, isn't it?" Alex jumped at Zephyr's voice, inches from his ear.

Alex shook his head to recover from the trance that the sight had evoked. "I'm not sure that 'beautiful' is a strong enough word to describe it."

Zephyr, a bit wistfully, replied, "I supposed I tend to take all this for granted. It's nice to see it through the eyes of an outsider for a change."

"Not a lot of visitors in Lumora?" Lucy asked, apparently drawn to the conversation beside her.

Auril gave a small snort. "You two're the first that I know of. The Cap'n has never brought anyone else back with 'im before."

Alex and Lucy shared a long look as they contemplated the implications of this revelation. Finally, still wide-eyed and slightly suspicious, Alex looked back at the two men. "Never? Not one guest in all this time?"

Auril looked Alex from head to toe, and back again. A small noise came from his throat, almost a growl, before speaking. "I can't see what makes 'ya special either, but it ain't my place to question the Cap'n."

Zephyr shot his elder an admonishing glare, then turned to Alex and Lucy, his eyes softening. "I understand you ran into some trouble out there. The Captain is a good man with a good sense of people. If he brought you here, it's because he felt you were good people who needed help." A small grunt earned Auril another sharp look from the younger guard. "Some of us, apparently, still don't quite understand that."

Auril returned the gaze only for a moment before bowing his head slightly and dropping back a step. Alex marked the odd juxtaposition that made him wonder about the hierarchy of the pairing. He had assumed that the older man would be the senior officer, but he had clearly been mistaken. The fact that this city seemed to value and respect kindness, even surrounded by an unforgiving world, made him think better of Lumora and pushed away some of the apprehension that had been nagging him since arriving.

Giving a quick nod and appreciative smile to Zephyr, Alex faced ahead once again to find that the entire marble palace was now in view. Before them, an ornate golden gate was already swinging open in anticipation of their arrival. The majestic banners and golden accents continued along the parapets and encased the archway, which housed two expertly carved wooden doors. Heavy, polished oak slabs, nearly double Alex's height, were adorned with gleaming iron hardware. The carvings were of two regal-looking lions reared up on their hind legs, their front paws meeting in the center as if waiting to open the doors for the group.

As if the lions themselves were listening to Alex's thoughts, the massive, heavy portals lurched slightly before swinging open smoothly and soundlessly, a testament to the master craftsmanship that could be observed throughout the city. There were no guards at the doors, so Alex assumed that there was a hidden mechanism to control them. Or perhaps it was the city's magic welcoming them inside. Alex filed that away as a question for a later time.

As they stepped within the grand entrance of the Lumoran royal castle, the grand foyer stood as an enchanting prelude to the artistic marvels that lay beyond its majestic doors. It was a chamber bathed in a soft, ethereal glow, where the very air seemed to hum with creativity and history. Beneath their feet, the floor was a tapestry of light, a river of luminous tiles that shimmered with an ever-shifting array of colors. It was as if the very ground was a living canvas, telling tales in pixels and hues.

Towering columns, adorned with intricate carvings and reliefs, lined the sides of the foyer. They reached toward the impossibly high arched ceiling as if telling a seemingly endless tale. These columns were not merely architectural; they were monuments to Lumoran reverence for art and culture, standing sentinel in cultural splendor.

Upon the walls, canvases came to life with brilliant, dancing colors. Lumoran royalty, great artists, and pivotal moments in history were immortalized in meticulous brushstrokes. Each piece was a masterful composition, a canvas of passion and storytelling, inviting viewers to lose themselves in its intricate details.

Suspended from the ceiling, crystal chandeliers cast a mesmerizing play of light on the floor. They were more than luminous fixtures; they were works of art in their own right, adding an air of magic and wonder to the space.

Throughout the foyer, statues and sculptures of Lumoran figures stood as silent witnesses to the passage of time. Their immortalized expressions conveyed a sense of wisdom, courage, and artistic fervor. They were guardians of Lumora's heritage, their presence a reminder of the profound connection between art and the soul of this city.

As the group moved through the foyer, their footsteps created echoes that reverberated harmoniously, as if the very space itself responded to their presence with a symphony of sound. The foyer seemed a living, breathing entity, welcoming those who entered with an orchestration of appreciation.

At the far end of this cultural wonderland, the regal double doors leading to the throne room stood in resplendent glory. These doors were not merely portals; they were works of art unto themselves, bearing finely carved depictions of Lumoran royals in regal poses. They beckoned visitors forward, promising the awe-inspiring artistic treasures that awaited within.

Alex and Lucy marveled at the city's rich history depicted on every surface around them, every step leading to a new expression of the cultural evolution of Lumora over countless centuries. As they walked, the doors at the end of the hall opened to reveal a well-dressed, older man. His suit was perfectly tailored to his slender build; dark gray pants, pressed and pleated to perfection, and a two-button jacket with wide lapels over a collarless white dress shirt that contrasted brilliantly with his shimmering, blue skin. The suit was of the finest fabric, vibrant with a satin-like sheen. When he spoke, it was with an air of authority, but not unkind. Giving a small bow to Helios, he said "She has been expecting you."

Helios gave a nod in return. "Thank you, Mr. Eventide."

The regal man attempted a stern look, though the upturned corners of his pursed lips betrayed him. "Please, sir. We've been over this on several occasions. Call me Lysander."

The Captain flashed a grin that led Alex and Lucy to believe that they were witnessing an inside joke that they were not privy to. "Of course, Mr. Eventide."

The man in the doorway grinned back, as if expecting that exact response, then shook his head in mock frustration. "You're going to be the reason I retire. You are aware of that, correct?"

As the group reached the end of the hall, Helios took the man's outstretched hand in greeting, a wide smile spreading across his bright face. "You're not going anywhere, old friend.

You know it as well as I do." Moments later, the smile faded as he leaned closer and lowered his voice. "Is she angry?"

Lysander, his voice barely above a whisper, replied "She doesn't seem to be. Then again, she is not the type to allow her emotions to betray her, is she?"

The Captain's face dropped as if he were a scolded child. "No, she certainly is not." Helios regained his composure before addressing the group behind him. "I suppose there shall be no more delay, then. Time to meet the Queen."

"The Queen?" Alex nearly choked on the words in surprise. "You're kidding, right?"

"Not at all, Alex." Helios replied. "No need for concern. If she's angry, it won't be at you."

A snort of muffled laughter came from their side where Aurora stood, trying to stifle a smile. "Don't worry. He's used to it."

Helios shot a look at Aurora that Alex couldn't quite read, then stiffened as he crossed the threshold to enter the throne room, taking on an air of formality. Phalen and Aurora followed suit behind him, matching his cadence as if rehearsed. Zephyr and Auril stayed behind, taking up stations on either side of the door.

The throne room was a sight to behold. It was grandiose, yet somehow intimate, with a sense of regal power that emanated from every corner. The walls were adorned with tapestries and paintings, each one telling a story of Lumora's past glories. The ceiling soared high above, painted with intricate designs that seemed to dance in the light of the chandeliers.

At the far end of the room sat the Queen herself, upon her throne of gold and velvet. She was a vision of elegance and grace, her regal bearing commanding respect from all who gazed upon her. Her eyes were piercing, seeming to see into the very souls of those before her.

As Helios approached, he dropped to one knee in deference to his monarch, Aurora, and Phalen mimicking the gesture behind him. "Your Majesty," he said, his voice filled with reverence and loyalty.

The Queen of Lumora was a portrait of poise and regal authority. Crowned with a diadem adorned with gems that caught the light in a dazzling display, her visage was one of serene majesty. She was draped in robes woven from the most exquisite blue fabrics, a cobalt only a shade or two lighter than her flawless, glowing skin. Her attire was a masterpiece of Lumoran craftsmanship, each thread bearing intricate patterns that told stories of Lumora's culture and creativity. Her attire seemed to shift and dance with the ambient light, a living canvas of Lumoran artistry.

The eyes of the Queen in front of them were glowing pools of wisdom and depth, seeming to hold the secrets of Lumora's past and the hopes of its future. The lines on her face showed her to be a woman wizened with age, though she bore the years well. Alex thought back to his neighbor, Mrs. Jones, as he recognized the face of a woman more prone to smiling than frowning, and he instantly liked her for that reason alone.

She nodded slightly as her gaze shifted to each of the guards kneeling in her presence, and then to Alex and Lucy as they followed suit. There was a slight apprehension in her eyes, of course, but there was also kindness. This was not a woman who ruled by fear. Alex let out a breath he didn't know he was holding at this realization.

There was a long silence as the Queen examined the small group in front of her. Finally, as her gaze settled on the Captain of the Lumoran Guard, her stoic expression softened to a look of amusement. "Would you please get up Helios?" Her voice rang out into the pristine acoustics of the throne room, a bit of a lilt throughout as if trying not to laugh. "You know very well that there is no need for such formality when addressing your own mother."

Eight

A Crisis of Conflux

Alex raised an eyebrow at this new information, sharing a look with Lucy that showed she had suspected Helios to have downplayed his importance as well.

"You did not tell them?" The Queen had caught the silent conversation between the newcomers. Alex had a feeling that she didn't miss much. She stood in a fluid, graceful motion that seemed almost ethereal. "Please, everyone rise."

"I felt it prudent to withhold certain details until we were safely within the city," Helios returned as he rose to his feet. He then turned to Alex and Lucy. "I apologize for the lack of transparency. I assure you, it was simply out of caution."

"I have a feeling, my dear Lios," the Queen flashed a sly grin at Lucy and Alex, "that apologies are not necessary in this instance."

The Captain of the Guard, and Prince of Lumora, looked back at his mother quizzically. "Why not?"

"Because, my son, you have many great talents, but

subterfuge is certainly not one of them. Unless I miss my guess, I suspect that our visitors have been on to you since before you entered the city."

"That's impossible. How could they have..." Helios trailed off as he glanced from face to face, at the smirks serving to confirm his mother's words. Smiles grew to laughter as his face turned a deep violet from the blush entering his cheeks.

When the laughter died down, the Queen regained her composure and stepped down from the dais where her ornate throne perched. She stepped forward and took Alex's hand in greeting. "Alex Porter, correct?" She then extended her free hand to Lucy. "And Lucy Watts?"

Alex and Lucy nodded, both taken aback by the fact that she already knew who they were.

"I am Queen Celestia Dawnwhisper Pixelhart. It is a pleasure to finally have you in our city." The smile she gave was genuine, almost relieved, and made her look far too young to have a son Helios' age. "Though I believe that I may have just lost my throne."

Alex looked behind the Queen to find that Whiskers had curled up in the plush seat atop the dais. "I am so sorry, Queen Celestia. I'll take care of..."

"No, it is quite alright, Alex," the Queen interjected. She then turned to address the feline in question. "You must be the infamous Whiskers." She bent down to give him a scratch behind the ear. "You are welcome to my seat, little one. Just don't scratch it up, understood?"

"*I sleep,*" Whiskers purred as his eyelids slowly closed.

Lucy took a tentative step forward, unsure of the protocols involved in royal interactions. "Queen Celestia, if I may ask..."

"How did I know you were coming?"

The Queen's bluntness briefly staggered Lucy. "Well... yeah... I mean, yes, and how do you know so much about us?"

"It's quite simple, really. I've been waiting for you to arrive for nearly a decade." Marking the instant confusion mirrored on the faces of all except her son, Queen Celestia continued. "You see, our city has been facing an ongoing crisis for many years. I'm sure you have been informed of our city's role in protecting the arts and culture of this world, yes? We are also the custodians of the Lumigenesis Conflux, the wellspring of this world's magic, from which all life originates in this land."

"Lumora is the last bastion of our former world. Generations ago, the lands of Luterre were full of cities just like this one. It was a time of great peace and prosperity. But, as time went on, the land became polluted and the magic weakened. Day after day, the Conflux has begun to flow more slowly, and will eventually run dry if we do not intervene."

"I don't mean to sound insensitive, your Majesty." Alex began carefully. "This sounds like a terrible situation for your people, and I am truly sorry for all that you've endured, but what does this have to do with us?"

"First, Alex, please call me Celestia. We are not so formal in this realm. Second, I understand your confusion, as I shared the same feeling for many years. When I was a child, my father would tell me stories of adventurers from another world, who would enter portals into our realm to complete quests. Obviously, I thought it was an absurd, frivolous fantasy. But then, the Lumigenesis Conflux began weakening and, with it, the veil between worlds. Stories began circulating of dangers passing through the crossing, a blight that destroyed cities, corrupted forests, tainted the wildlife and people. I was still very young when my father set out with his guard to investigate."

The end of the story remained unspoken, but the sadness in the Queen's eyes said volumes. Helios moved to stand beside his mother, laying a hand on her shoulder.

Everyone in the room was hesitant to break the silence, but Alex had to be sure he understood. "So you're saying that your world and ours are bleeding together?"

Celestia gave a small nod, her eyes still glistening with unshed tears. "And both realms are suffering greatly for it."

Alex thought for a moment. "And where does our quest come in to all this?"

"Yes, the Teapot of Destiny, correct?" the Queen shrugged and gestured to a serving cart next to the wall, an ornate tea set arranged on the tray. "A ruse, I am afraid, to start you on your journey."

"So you lobotomized my neighbor, just to get me here?" Alex's tone was sharp. He didn't like being manipulated, especially at the expense of Mrs. Jones.

"No, Alex. Of course not. That poor woman had already been taken by the corruption. I truly wish we didn't have to use her misfortune to our advantage, but it was the only way to get our message through."

Lucy stepped forward then. "Your Majes... Celestia," she amended after receiving an admonishing look from the Queen, "it would benefit all of us to work together to fix this. That much is perfectly clear. But you haven't explained yet how the two of us, specifically, fit into all this."

"Of course. Apologies, my dear. The last city fell a decade

ago, leaving only Lumora as a safe haven for those of us who were left. It was a much smaller city at the time, so the outskirts were littered with refugee encampments. We did everything we could, but we just didn't have the resources to help everyone. One such refugee was a human man from your world. Unfortunately, we were unable to save him, but before he passed, he told us of two great heroes who would one day find themselves in our world. Two heroes of unmatched bravery, unrivaled cleverness and skill. He told us of you, Xyra." Her eyes met Lucy's with unwavering belief, then shifted to Alex. "And of you, Nexxus."

The room went quiet once again. Alex and Lucy looked at each other, then back to Celesta. Finally, their eyes met once again. This time, it was Lucy who broke the silence. "Nexxus?" Her voice was a near whisper in disbelief.

"You're... Xyra?" Alex stared in astonishment.

Alex shook his head as he attempted to take in the information that had been unloaded on them. "Queen Celestia, I think there has been a huge misunderstanding. Nexxus is just a video game character that I control. I'm not equipped to save two worlds. I'm nobody."

Celestia stepped in front of Alex and lifted his chin until their eyes met. The look she gave him was gentle and motherly, but there was a quiet strength to it. It was easy to see how Helios became the man he was, having this woman raise him. "It is your mind behind that character, Alex. Your intelligence that solves his problems. Your knowledge that propagates his skill. It is your focus that drives his ambition. You are far more than you think you are." She stopped to shift so she could address Lucy as well. "Both of you are far more than you think you are. We did not seek you out for your arsenal of weaponry, your speed, your strength, or any of that nonsense. We sought you out because you have heroic hearts and keen minds."

The Queen of Lumora stepped away, gesturing around the room at the thousands of carvings and canvases surrounding them. It was the entire history of this wondrous city, laid before them in artistic representation. "We are not a city of warriors. We are a city of thinkers, of dreamers, of believers. That is what we need if we are to seal this rift; if we are to save our two worlds from collapse."

Standing before them was no mere ruler. Celestia Dawnwhisper Pixelhart was a queen in every sense of the word. She was a leader, an inspiration, a teacher, a mother, and a friend to her people. Not only to her people, it seemed, for as Alex and Lucy stood in awe of the resplendent, powerful woman before them, neither could help but believe in her with the same passion as the citizens of this city did.

As Alex stood beside his recent companion, facing the magnificent ruler of a city of dreams, he felt his resolve strengthen, surrounding him like an impenetrable suit of armor. He felt strong, powerful, everything he never believed himself to be. "Well then, Queen Celestia," he began with a renewed determination, "where do we begin?"

The bright smile of the monarch was everything he had hoped for when he spoke those words. However, he did not expect to see a very different smile on Lucy's face when he turned to meet her sparkling emerald eyes. If he didn't know any better, he may have believed it to be admiration. Alex felt an unexpected warmth in his chest at the sight, and for once in his life, he began to think he may finally have something worth fighting for.

When Alex and Lucy looked back to the Queen, she met them with a small smirk that implied she was fully aware of every unspoken thought that had transpired between them in that moment. She gave a small sigh before speaking. "I believe that our first course of action should be a hot meal and an evening's rest. I trust you two could use both, after the trials you've faced recently."

She then gave them a look that was anything but queenly. "Perhaps some time for the two of you in a more comfortable environment will be... illuminating?" Her eyebrows raised at this last word and her tone held all the implications that she left unsaid. Seeing the perturbed expression cross Helios' face, she continued. "Come now, Lios. How do you think you got here?" With a small laugh that was wholly unexpected from the regal woman, Celestia wordlessly turned and exited into the foyer.

"Mother!" Helios gasped incredulously, the not-so-subtle innuendo coming from his mother and queen nearing on traumatic. Her only response, a quickening of her melodious laughter, reverberated throughout the immaculate acoustics of the room.

Lysander appeared in the doorway almost immediately after the Queen's departure. "She certainly seemed to be in a good mood." His smile dropped slightly as he noticed the disturbed look on the Captain's face. "What did I miss?"

"Nothing I'd ever want repeated, Lysander."

"Lumos help us." Lysander put a perfectly manicured hand to his chest in mock surprise. "If you're too traumatized to ignore my request to use my given name, whatever was said must have come as quite a shock."

Lucy looked at him with visible strain, attempting to stifle her laughter at Helios' unease. "I believe our friend here," gesturing toward Helios, "has never been forced to see his mother as a woman before."

Lysander gave a grin that implied he knew exactly what was said, and was truly enjoying the Captain's discomfort. "Sir, she truly is quite the..."

Helious' eyes darted toward his friend. "Do not finish that sentence. Ever."

Lysander's eyes glimmered with amusement as his grin widened. Finally, his eyes shifted toward Alex and Lucy. "Mr. Porter, Ms. Watts, I have been asked to show you to the guest chambers so you can rest and freshen up before dinner. Please follow me."

Alex smiled back at the Lysander. "Thank you, Mr. Eventide. We would greatly appreciate that."

Lysander sighed deeply. "Please, not you too. Lysander, if you will."

Alex flashed a grin at Helios that helped him shake off his previous distress. "Of course," he gave a mocking bow, complete with hand flourish, "Mr. Eventide."

"Oh, dear Lumos," Lysander said quietly, before turning on his heel and leaving the room.

With a chuckle, Helios turned to the two newcomers. "You may want to follow. He's quick for an old man."

"My hearing is still flawless as well." Lysander's voice echoed from the foyer.

Lucy and Alex bid a short farewell to their new friends

and followed Lysander into the foyer, leaving a reverberation of hearty laughter behind them.

Nine

Home Is Where the Heart Is

Alex stood in awe of the grand guest quarters he had been offered. The chamber was bathed in a gentle, ever-changing glow. The walls were adorned with tapestries depicting the artistic history of Lumora, their vibrant colors shifting and dancing in response to the light.

At the center of the room, a magnificent canopy bed stood draped with sheer woven fabrics of various hues. Its headboard bore intricate, scrolling designs that disappeared behind soft pillows of fine silk. A luxurious quilt beckoned invitingly, promising a warm and comfortable rest from the moment he touched it.

Lumora's rich cultural tradition was on full display within the chamber. To the left of the bed stood an easel prepared with a blank canvas, and in the corner next to that, a beautiful writing desk stocked with pens, multiple inkwells, and a stack of parchment. The corner to the right held various musical instruments, including a piano and multiple percussive, wind, and stringed instruments, many of which Alex only vaguely recognized.

Opposite the exquisite bed stood two towering bookshelves, which framed the large glass doors leading to the private balcony. Stained glass panes in intricate patterns cast a colorful hue along the chamber floor as he approached.

Alex ran his hands along the spines of the tomes filling the massive shelves. The Alchemist's Palette, The Chromatic Chronicles, Brushstrokes of Lumora. "I should probably learn something about this place, if I'm going to help save it," he said to himself, choosing a tome from the shelves that caught his eye.

Alex seated himself in one of the overstuffed chairs in the reading nook, while Whiskers had nestled into the chair he had claimed opposite Alex. He was well into chapter two of Canvas of Whispers: The Secrets of Lumora's Art, when he was interrupted by a knock at the door.

Using the ribbon attached to the binding, he marked his page and set the book on a nearby table. "Who could that be?" he asked Whiskers.

Whiskers seemed far too comfortable to care, so Alex crossed the room to open the door, revealing Helios finely attired in his dress uniform.

"Good evening Alex." He looked within to see Whiskers stretching lazily on the soft cushion of the chair. "I see that your friend has settled in well."

Alex nodded in agreement. "Whiskers has never had a

problem getting comfortable. To what may I owe the pleasure, Prince?"

"Captain, please," Helios replied curtly.

Alex was a bit confused by the reaction. "Your mother is queen. Doesn't that make you a prince?"

"Technically, yes, but it's not..." He looked away, deep in thought. "Let's just say that I earned my position as captain. That is who I am."

Alex nodded, "Captain it is, then."

"Thank you." Helios sighed, as if relieved to not have to explain further. "Oh, of course! I have come to inform you that dinner is nearly ready. My mother requested that I inform you of the wardrobe in your chambers. You will find it fully furnished with any clothing you might require. Fair warning though, my mother takes formal dinners very seriously. Choose wisely."

The Captain gave a light chuckle at the fear-stricken look on Alex's face before he wordlessly turned and walked down the hall. Alex closed the door slowly before turning to find Whiskers looking back at him, head cocked slightly. "*Food?*" the bubble communicated over his head.

"Of course you heard that part. I'm sure they'll have something for you too, buddy."

The dreaded wardrobe stood to his left, nestled between Whiskers' chair and the door to a personal washroom. He eyed the wardrobe suspiciously, as if it were going to attack. "I should probably wash up first. After, we can figure out what counts as 'dinner formal' in this world."

Alex was startled as the sound of running water immediately echoed from the washroom. Upon entering, he found a large shower stall of chiseled slate tile, perfectly tempered water raining down from an indiscernible location.

"Right, magic." The realization, however, did not diminish the awe he felt at such an immediate response to his need. "I could get used to this."

Alex quickly showered and dried, then searched the wardrobe. To his astonishment, every article of clothing seemed tailored to him. The entire collection was filled with his favorite colors and styles, and each piece fit as if made for him. He finally settled on a similar outfit to the one he saw Lysander wearing earlier, a navy suit pinstriped with silver thread, and a collarless dress shirt in a pale salmon color.

"How do I look, Whiskers? Fit to dine with royalty?"

Whiskers blinked back at him for a moment before a bubble appeared over his head. "*Food now?*"

"Yeah, that's what I thought. Come on, let's see if we can find the dining room."

Alex left the room, his furry companion following on his heels, and began to descend the grand staircase to the foyer below.

Lysander stood at the bottom of the stairs, nodding in approval. "Mr. Porter, excellent choice. She will be pleased."

"I'm glad the Queen will approve. I wasn't sure what would be appropriate for a royal dinner."

Lysander gave a small chuckle. "Yes, her too. Come, I will show you to the dining hall."

Perplexed, Alex began to ask who else he meant, but soon realized that he was being left behind. Lysander had no intention of explaining further.

Alex wasn't sure what he expected from the dining hall

of the Lumoran palace, but the room he was led to was far from anything he could have anticipated. Compared to the elaborate, vaulted rooms he had seen previously, the dining hall was surprisingly small and intimate.

The room was a perfect circle, with a table to match in the center. The scene was reminiscent of the King Arthur legends Alex used to adore as a child, a room where everyone was equal. There was no head of this table, all the chairs the same beautifully carved dark oak.

Sconces lined the circumference of the room, candlelight casting a warm glow against the glistening marble walls. A fixture hanging above the table shone with an ethereal, soft glow to complement the yellows and oranges of the flames. Opposite the door, there was a massive fireplace, the hearth at least five feet from the floor. The fire roaring within the stone fireplace added a warmth to the room, greeting its guests as if they were family.

Queen Celestia and Captain Helios were already seated on either side of the hearth, breaking from their conversation as he entered. "Alex, you look wonderful," Queen Celestia greeted him. "Salmon suits you. An excellent choice."

"Thank you, your Ma..." an admonishing look from the woman made him rethink his words. "Celestia."

A warm smile returned to the Queen's face as she gestured toward the table. "Please take a seat. Lucy should be down at any moment." She then turned to the entryway where Lysander still stood. "Could you please make sure she finds her way, Lysander?"

"Of course, your Majesty," he replied with a small bow, before returning to the hall beyond and out of sight.

Alex chose a seat next to Helios, placing his hands awkwardly in his lap. "I'm sorry," he said nervously. "I really don't know the etiquette for something like this."

Helios let out a hearty laugh as he clapped Alex on the back. "Relax, Alex. It's just a meal, not a royal wedding." His jaw went slack as his eyes drifted to the door. Cocking a bushy eyebrow back at Alex, he continued. "Though that could be arranged, if the need arises."

"What are you..." Alex's voice trailed off as he turned and saw the reason for Helios' change in disposition.

Lucy stood framed by the arched entry, flickers of firelight dancing along her face. Her eyes glimmered as if true emeralds had been set within them, the effect enhanced further by the dazzling smile on her ruby lips as her eyes met his. She brushed a tendril of her short, black hair from her face as she looked away shyly.

She wore a sleeveless, steel-gray dress that fit her form like a second skin, flaring slightly just below her hips into an asymmetrical skirt cut from mid-thigh on her left to nearly floor length on the right. A thick leather belt, adorned with silver embellishments, hung loosely around her waist, and the scooped neck of the dress was accentuated by a thin silver chain holding a brilliantly cut green stone that matched her eyes perfectly.

Alex rose to his feet as if pulled by invisible strings, his mind racing to find words. In a trance, he moved within reach of Lucy before he knew what he was doing.

Lucy looked back at him, her face dropping slightly. "Are you going to say something?"

Alex continued to look into her deep green eyes. He opened his mouth to speak, but no words would come.

"I look ridiculous, don't I? I knew I should have..."

Panicked, Alex interrupted. "No! No, absolutely not! You look..." he searched for a word that was strong enough to convey what he saw before him, but none existed. "You look incredible."

He was rewarded with a brilliant smile that lit her face in a way he didn't realize he was longing to see. "You clean up pretty well yourself, Nexxus." Her smile turned to a mocking grin with the last word.

Alex looked at the ground, heat creeping in his cheeks. "I just... the clothes are..."

"Don't do that, Alex." Lucy placed a finger under his chin, lifting his face to look at her. "You look great. Take the compliment."

"Apologies for the intrusion." Celestia's voice rang through the room. "This is truly entertaining to watch, but I am famished." She gestured to the table, which had been set with several dishes and platters during their interaction. "Shall we?"

Alex could feel the blush still on his cheeks as he pulled a chair from the table, offering it to Lucy before retaking his own seat between her and Helios. The Captain leaned in toward Alex and spoke quietly, barely above a whisper. "Quite the charmer, I see."

The venomous look Alex shot back was betrayed by the embarrassment still evident on his face, eliciting a chuckle from Helios.

Queen Celestia stood, once everyone was settled at the

table. "Alex, Lucy, thank you both for joining us for dinner. We have much to discuss, but for now, that can wait. You must be starving after everything you've been through. Please," she lifted a delicate, bejeweled hand, and a blue orb of pure light formed around her outstretched fingers, "eat first, then we speak."

She swept her glowing hand over the table and the light released in a shower of sparks. The platters and serving ware sprang to life, filling everyone's plates with foods that Alex didn't entirely recognize, but smelled amazing. His stomach growled in response, a hunger that he hadn't fully realized until this moment.

The food tasted as good as it smelled. Spices and flavors that Alex had never experienced before danced along his palette, and he found himself eating until he felt he was about to burst.

"That was the most amazing meal I've ever had," Lucy said, addressing the Queen. "Thank you so much for the hospitality you've shown us."

Alex nodded as he echoed the sentiment. "Yes, we truly appreciate everything you've done for us."

Celestia beamed proudly. "You are most welcome for the invitation, but I'm afraid I cannot take credit for the hospitality. The Palace is happiest when those she chooses to serve are happy."

"She chooses?" Alex was taken aback by the notion. "You mean to tell us that this palace is... alive?"

"Do you not feel it? She takes care of us, feeds and warms us, as she has every generation since she was built. In fact, some say she was not built at all, but simply arrived one day, a gift from the Mother."

Alex stopped for a moment to take in the surrounding palace. He felt a warmth surround him, not simply from the fireplace, but a sort of ethereal embrace like a mother's touch. As a serene smile marked his face, he saw the Queen nod in approval.

"You do. I see it in your eyes."

"So the shower, the wardrobe..." Alex mused.

"Lights, fire, food... all her," Helios interjected.

"But, how?" Lucy asked.

"You see," Queen Celestia began, "the Lumigenesis Conflux resides in a cavern just below our feet. It is the palace's heart, its soul, and the palace is its protector. They exist to serve each other, and us as their stewards."

As she spoke, the lighting dimmed noticeably, and a chill swept through the chamber. Within seconds, the room was once again bright and warm, but the memory of the chill remained in their eyes.

Helios frowned as he broke the silence. "Unfortunately, as the Conflux suffers this blight, so does the palace. These episodes are becoming more and more frequent."

Lucy rose from her seat, placing a hand on the warm marble of the wall. "So she's... she's dying?"

This time, it was Celestia's turn to frown. "In a manner of speaking, yes."

Lucy looked back at the table. "What can we do to fix this?"

"That, my dear, is what we are here to discuss."

Ten

Flirtations, Frustrations, and Revelations

"Do you understand what you're asking of us?" Lucy asked, her arms folded neatly over her chest as she eyed the Queen.

"I do." Celestia nodded slightly. "I understand the monumental request I put before you both. I wish it were not necessary, but this is our final hope to end this blight."

"Helios," Alex pleaded, "you said you've lost how many guards?"

The Captain looked away as he answered. "Fifteen."

"Fifteen people, all sent out to investigate the blight. None returned. That is what you expect the two of us to..."

"Three," Helios interjected.

"Lios!" A mix of shock and fear flashed across the Queen's face.

"Mother, I cannot allow them to go alone!" His eyes darted to his mother's face, then slowly turned back to Alex and Lucy. "When I found the two of you, I thought I had simply found the heroes foreseen in our histories. I did not expect, in such a short time, to find two people who I consider to be friends. If you do not wish to endanger yourselves for us, I cannot fault you for that. But if you can find it within you. If you can find the courage to aid our cause, you will not be alone." Once again, he turned to his mother. "Those in my charge have sacrificed for this. I can do no less."

Lucy looked between the two royals for a moment. "Well, if nothing else, you Lumorans are excellent motivational speakers." She gave a somber smile that didn't quite reach her eyes, her attempt at a joke falling flat in the seriousness of the situation. "I think we need to discuss things before making any decisions. I can't speak for Alex, but I want to help. I'm just not sure how I can."

"Yes, of course," the Queen stood as she spoke. "I do not wish for you to make such an important decision on impulse. My son and I may not agree on all matters, but I have grown rather fond of you as well. I am ashamed to say that I did not expect so much kindness, caring, and understanding from humans. It has been far more difficult than I had hoped to ask so much of you. Take the time you need. Talk amongst your-selves. In fact," her attention turned to Helios for a moment before continuing, her expression not entirely kind, "I believe my son and I must have a discussion as well."

Alex and Lucy stood in unison, both giving small bows as they bid good evening to their hosts. They were nearly out the door when Celestia's voice trailed after them.

"If I may be so bold," the pair turned as the Queen addressed them, "I would ask a favor of you both. Tomorrow morning, I would like you to join me in the Conflux chamber to see what we are fighting against. However, I would ask that tonight, you spend some time outside of these walls. See the city, meet its people. Find out what it is that we are fighting for."

Alex smiled at the request. "I've been dying to see more of your city since we first stepped through the gates."

"Same here. Anything special we should see?" Lucy added.

Helios thought for a moment. "One of my favorite places in the city has always been Sonata Square. You'll know it when you hear it," he said with a smile. " I will send for Aurora to accompany you. This is a peaceful city, but some people get nervous around new faces in times like this. Plus, she won't stop talking about that rescue at the woods. I think you have a fan, Lucy."

Lucy's face reddened slightly. "Me? You saved our asses back there. I didn't do anything."

"That's not how she's been telling it. That's not how any of us saw it. You were the hero. We were just there to back you up."

Lucy looked incredulously at Alex, but he simply smiled back at her, nodding in agreement. "He's not wrong. I wouldn't have made it out of that treeline if it weren't for you."

Her already pink cheeks turned scarlet at the praise, and she turned away to hide her embarrassment. "Let's go take that walk," she said quietly, walking out the door with Alex trailing behind her.

***

Alex and Lucy stood within the palace gates as Aurora arrived. She had forgone the familiar guard uniform, opting instead for a pair of loose-fitting black slacks and a white, floral print top. The sleeves of her blouse billowed around her upper arm before cinching just below the elbow, leaving her strong, toned forearms in plain view. The tight braids she wore while on duty had been let down to reveal thick black hair that fell just past her shoulder in loose waves.

Lucy stepped forward at her approach, smiling broadly. "Wow, you look fantastic. No uniform tonight?"

"Me?" Aurora scoffed. "Next to you two, I look like a scullery maid. The Captain asked me to keep a low profile tonight. Close enough to keep you safe, but not so imposing that people keep their distance."

Lucy grinned. "I hate to be the bearer of bad news, Aurora, but you're going to intimidate a lot of people looking like that."

Aurora flashed a sultry look. "Oh, I'm aware. And my friends call me Rori."

Lucy laughed, a melodious sound that reverberated through the courtyard. "Well then Rori, care to show us around your city?"

Aurora beamed back at her. "I'd be honored."

As the trio ventured into the enchanting streets of Lumora, the city seemed to come alive under the night sky. Enchanted lanterns illuminated the cobblestone paths, casting an ethereal glow that danced on the facades of the surrounding buildings. The air was filled with the sweet melodies of

     T. Penyor Reed

distant musicians, each note harmonizing with the next, a serenade of Lumora's creative spirit.

Sonata Square awaited, and it didn't take long for them to follow the rich, symphonic sounds to find it. As they entered, the quiet streets gave way to a bustling city square. Even in the late hour, the paved cul-de-sac brimmed with musicians, painters, and performers of all kinds showcasing their talents. The captivating notes of a street violinist's melody wafted through the air, setting the perfect backdrop for the captivating surroundings.

Lucy's eyes sparkled with curiosity as she took in the sights and sounds. She leaned closer to Aurora and asked, "Is it always like this? It's incredible."

Aurora nodded, her own appreciation of the scene evident. "Oh, absolutely. This square is always alive with music and creativity, a place where anyone can express themselves freely."

Wide-eyed, Alex took in cultural utopia. "This is... perfect." He looked at Lucy with a newfound determination. "We can't let this die, can we?"

Lucy met his eyes with a similar sense of purpose. "No, I don't think we can."

Aurora smiled, motioning to the center of the square. "You haven't seen anything yet." She placed a hand on each of their backs and gently pushed them toward the bustling festival.

Alex's heart raced as they entered Sonata Square, the vibrant and captivating atmosphere enveloping them. As they took in the variety of performances, he couldn't help but notice the exchanges between Lucy and Aurora. Their smiles, their laughter, and the way they interacted carried a playful energy. It was undeniable that there was a connection between them, a connection that stirred something inside him that he didn't particularly like.

As they strolled through the bustling square, the music beckoned them closer to the talented violinist. Lucy was drawn to the music like a moth to a flame, her eyes alight with curiosity. She swayed gently to the melody, and Alex watched in awe of her grace and enthusiasm. He appreciated her zest for life and her ability to find joy in the little things.

Lucy whirled around once, twice, then came to a stop, an arm outstretched to Alex. "Join me?"

Alex gave her a bemused look. "Really? You're asking me?"

Lucy laughed. "Well, I'm certainly not going to wait all night for you to ask me."

Alex took her hand tentatively. "I'm not much of a dancer."

"Just feel the music and follow my lead," Lucy replied.

Alex didn't quite recognize the style of the music, but it was something akin to a fast waltz. Simple enough to follow, as long as you didn't mix up the count. Which, of course, he did... multiple times. As he held Lucy in his arms, his hand resting on the bare skin exposed by her backless dress, his focus wavered considerably.

Lucy's laughter filled the air as he tripped for the third time, drawing the attention of other festival-goers. The allure of her infectious joy and the way her eyes sparkled with delight seemed to draw people in, much as it had drawn him to her. He admired her ability to connect with people and create a sense of warmth and camaraderie.

As the dance continued, the two began to find their

rhythm together, their bodies pressing close and moving as one. They turned in circles as the music enshrouded them, and the world lost focus, fading to nothing but streaks of color and light. They were the only two who existed in that moment, and Alex found himself wishing it could last forever.

Lucy's breath was labored, the sound overtaking the fading music and the crowds that Alex had forgotten. His breath had stopped completely. This moment. This was his chance. He leaned closer, gazing into the sparkling green eyes that he had grown to miss, to yearn for every time the two were apart. Mere inches away, he moved further, his lips brushing Lucy's lightly.

Suddenly, the moment was lost. Lucy pulled away sharply, leaving Alex off balance and confused. "I'm... I'm sorry, Alex... I just... can't..."

Alex was mortified. What was he thinking? "No, no... I'm the one who should be... I just got lost in..."

"Sorry guys." Aurora's voice cut through the tension as she walked up. "I ran into a friend of mine and got to talking. So, did I miss anything?"

Alex just shook his head, eyes fixed firmly on the ground at his feet. Lucy simply mumbled, "No, nothing."

"So... I missed something, but nobody's going to tell me. No worries, I don't need to know if you don't want to tell me. But we're here to have fun, so whatever it is, shake it off, and let's keep moving."

Rori guided them through the crowd, introducing them to the various artists and performers who called Sonata Square home. Alex watched as she worked her way through the crowd with a charisma and charm that he had always dreamed of having. More doubt crept into his mind as he realized that she was a faultless complement to Lucy's magnetic personality. Rori's presence added an extra layer of excitement to their evening, but for Alex, it also added feelings of envy that he wished he could subdue.

Alex's thoughts were interrupted when he felt a hand on his arm. A young woman, pale blue in complexion save for the slight pink of her cheeks, looked back at him as he turned. She was pretty, in a way that young women are when they have only recently left childhood. Her brown eyes were wide and innocent.

Her strawberry blonde hair hung loose over her right shoulder, and she swept it back in a dramatic flourish as she spoke softly. "I saw what happened. I'm so sorry."

Alex smiled politely. "It's okay. Thank you, though."

"I'm Astrid," she said, a shy smile spreading across her face. "I've heard the stories. I know who you are and why you're here. Thank you for helping us. It's so brave of you."

"Well, I haven't…"

Astrid continued, interrupting him. "I think some girls don't understand strong, smart guys like you. I think maybe they're intimidated by you, but I'm not like them."

"No, I bet you're not." Lucy flashed a sweetly venomous smile at Astrid as she stepped beside Alex. Astrid's smile faded as Lucy turned to Alex. "Are you ready? We're going to find a place to sit for a while."

Alex nodded, then turned back to Astrid. "It was really nice to meet you, Astrid. Have a great night." He gave her another polite smile as he turned and followed Lucy through the square.

As the crowds finally parted and they reached a charming café nestled beneath the elegant arches of the square, Alex pretended not to notice the playful teasing and flirtation between Lucy and Rori. He tried to ignore every exchange of knowing glances and light-hearted banter, or at least he pretended to. He was failing miserably to shut out their growing connection with each passing moment, and it made his earlier blunder all the more embarrassing.

Alex found himself caught in a whirlwind of emotion. He had grown fond of Lucy in the short time they had known each other. Her intelligence and wit, and her unwavering strength, had drawn him to her. But she deserved someone on her level, and he couldn't deny the chemistry he witnessed between Rori and Lucy. Aurora Artisynth was a force of nature that he had no chance of competing with.

And what he had done when they were dancing... he should have known better. They had been bound by circumstance, and it had become a foundation for a strong friendship, but that's all it was. Why would she ever want him? And now, the only real connection he'd ever felt could very well be ruined beyond repair. It was a bitter realization, a reminder that their adventure had brought them into a world where unexpected connections and attractions could blossom, and one wrong move could bring the world crashing down around him.

"So..." Alex turned to Lucy, eyes still lowered. "Thanks... you know... for helping me get out of there. With Astrid, I mean. I didn't know what to say."

"Yeah, I bet," she said flatly. "Don't worry about it."

Alex found himself even more confused by the response than he had been previously. Was that... jealousy? But why? She didn't want him. She made that clear when she walked away.

"Alex?" Aurora's voice cut through the thoughts that had invaded his mind.

"Oh, um, yeah?"

"I asked what you think of our city."

"Oh, sorry..." Shaking free from the distraction, he replied, "This city is unlike anything I could ever have imagined. It almost makes me wonder if I should abandon the search for the portal back home."

Lucy leaned in, looking concerned. "But wouldn't people wonder what happened to you? Friends? Family?" Her eyes turned away as she continued quietly, "Girlfriend?"

Alex laughed, more bitterly than he had meant to. "Girlfriend? No. No friends, unless you count the people I've met online. My parents are gone. Back home, I'm nothing and I have nobody. Here... well, I'm probably still nobody but..."

"You have to know that's not true!" Lucy snapped, the indignation in her voice causing Alex to jump in surprise.

"I just..." Alex attempted.

"Do you remember what you said to me earlier? About the woods? You wouldn't have made it without me? Alex, we would never have made it that far without you! I was ready to panic, and you kept me calm and grounded. I held on at the end because you inspired me to."

"She told me everything, Alex," Aurora interjected calmly, less the charmer they had come to know and more the protector they had first met. "I've served with men who folded under the same pressure that you thrived under in those woods. I've stood shoulder to shoulder with guards who panicked in similar situations where you stayed calm and worked the problem. You are not now, nor have you ever been nobody, and you are absolutely not alone any longer."

Alex sat and smiled at the two women in front of him, but said nothing. He could think of nothing that would express the gratitude he felt at that moment. The night in Sonata Square opened a door to a world of possibilities and emotions, leaving Alex to grapple with the complexities of his heart. But for the first time in his life, he felt like he could actually make a difference to someone.

Eleven

Resonant Regrets

The silver glow of the waxing moon shone from high overhead as the trio made their way back to the palace gates. The night had been a whirlwind of sensations, leaving Alex grappling with a complex mixture of emotions he couldn't easily untangle. Still, the purpose of the night had been fulfilled. He had seen the city, met the people, learned what was at stake, and he had fallen in love with all of it.

The sound of Lucy's laughter still lingered in his mind, and their dance was a haunting memory that he couldn't shake. It had been one of the best nights of his life, but also one of the worst.

Aurora had been a lively addition to their night. Her personality had made her the perfect guide for the night, introducing them to dozens of kind, warm Lumorans and their incredible talents. She had shown them a side of Lumora that sparkled with artistic fervor and welcomed them with open arms. Though her flirtation with Lucy and his disastrous misstep left Alex feeling like a third wheel, he couldn't bring himself to resent her for that. It was his own foolishness that led to his folly.

Lucy, who had been mostly quiet on the way back, finally broke the silence, her voice soft and laden with tension. "Tonight was... something, wasn't it?"

Alex nodded, his gaze locked on the cobbled path beneath their feet. "It was." He hesitated, the words dancing on the tip of his tongue before he decided against speaking his thoughts aloud.

Lucy, catching his hesitation, pressed on. "And the dance? You surprised me, Alex. I didn't think you had it in you."

Alex's lips curled into a half-smile. "I think I just got lost in the moment. You were amazing out there. I was just following your lead." Alex looked down at the cobblestone of the path before continuing. "Lucy, I really am..."

"Don't, Alex. Please don't apologize again. I can't bear to..." Lucy let out a deep sigh, attempting to hide the shaking in her voice. "There's nothing to apologize for, Alex."

Aurora stopped just short of the gate and looked from Alex to Lucy, then back again. "Okay, I need to ask. What exactly did you..." Finally, realization dawned on her face as she noticed the deep blush on Alex's cheeks. "Oh... oh, right. Forget I asked. Not my business, sorry."

An awkward silence followed, lingering for several moments before Aurora spoke again. "Well, it's getting late and I have morning duty, so I must be off. Have a good evening. Hopefully, I'll see you tomorrow."

Lucy embraced Rori as if they had known each other for

years. "Thank you so much for sharing your city with us. It was an incredible evening."

Alex worked to repress the pang of jealousy the embrace caused him, forcing a smile as he spoke. "Yes, thank you, Aurora. The city is more than I've ever dreamed of."

"Rori, remember? Friends call me Rori. I'm glad I got to be your guide tonight. It was fun." She then stepped to Alex's side. She laid her hand on his shoulder and lowered her voice next to his ear. "Please, remember what I said. You are a rare person, Alex Porter. A strong person. Much stronger than you know. I can only hope to be nearby when you finally figure that out." With those parting words, Aurora gave a small wave and walked toward the barracks.

Alex shrugged. "I'm getting pretty tired too, and we're probably going to have a lot to do tomorrow if we intend to save the world and all." A half-hearted chuckle was all he could muster. "Goodnight," he said shyly, turning to walk toward the Palace.

"Alex, please. You need to know..."

Alex stopped and looked back to interrupt. "Lucy, you don't need to explain anything. I get it. I just hope I didn't ruin our friendship with a stupid mistake." He turned back and continued walking, looking over his shoulder only to say "Goodnight Lucy."

He didn't look back again. He didn't know if he could bear it. If she was angry with him, it would hurt too much. If she was crying, it would destroy him. If she was neither, it would prove that he meant nothing to her. No good could come from looking back, so he continued to move forward.

Alex walked through the halls absently, the usual majesty

of the art and architecture lost on him as his mind wandered through the night's events.

"Alex, just the man I've been waiting for."

Alex looked up from the stairs he was ascending to find Helios standing outside his chamber door. "What can I do for you, Captain?"

"We need to talk, Alex. Can I come in?" Helios gestured to the door.

"I'm not sure I'd be very good company tonight, Helios. Is it something we could discuss in the morning?"

Helios shook his head slightly, looking somber. "I'm afraid not. I believe you need all the facts before you enter the Conflux chamber tomorrow."

Reaching the top of the stairs, Alex stopped to look at the Captain for a moment. Finally, he nodded wordlessly and opened the door.

Even in his dismal mood, Alex's face brightened as Whiskers padded across the room toward him. His furry companion rubbed against his leg, purring softly as if he knew that Alex needed him. "*Okay?*"

"Better now, buddy. Thank you."

Whiskers purred louder in response. "*I help?*"

"You always help, my friend," Alex replied with a smile.

Alex walked to the reading nook, taking the seat he had previously occupied before dinner. He looked to Helios, gesturing over the small table to a matching sofa across from him.

The Captain took the seat offered to him. "You've been doing some reading, I see."

Alex looked down at the table, to the forgotten copy of

Canvas of Whispers. "This place is fascinating. I wanted to learn more."

Helios nodded errantly. "Knowledge is good. Knowledge is power. Knowledge is..." He trailed off, obviously reluctant to brooch the topic of his visit. "Knowledge is why I'm here, I suppose. I'm sure you probably noticed some..." He shrugged slightly, searching for the right word. "Some resistance, shall we say, from my mother earlier. I need you to understand why, because I fear you may have the wrong idea about her intentions. You see, I was never meant to be Crown Prince. I had a brother once. Older, wiser, stronger than I could ever hope to be. Aureon would have been a truly impressive king one day, much like my father."

The Captain's eyes glistened, threatening to release the tears that he worked so hard to hold back. "You remind me of him. Of them both. In my youth and ignorance, I never appreciated them as I should have. I wasn't even there the day they set off to..." His voice cracked as he fought to keep his composure. "I was arrogant, hot-headed. I had no interest in the politics of this world. All I wanted to do was drink and fight. It's why I joined the guard. Well, that and to go against my father's wishes." Helios went silent again, his eyes unfocused as if watching a scene unfold that only he was privy to.

Alex waited patiently, not wanting to rush his friend's obvious grief and regret. After several moments, Helios took a deep breath and continued. "I wasn't there, because I had defied him. We fought, and I left. The next morning, my father and Aureon led a small contingent of guards to investigate the blight. They never returned. I never had the chance to apologize, to make things right. I never told my brother how much I admired him. My mother lost the love of her life and her eldest child, and I became Crown Prince on the back of my greatest shame."

"Helios," Alex breathed softly as realization dawned on him. "That's why you go by Captain, isn't it?" Alex sighed deeply with sorrow for his new friend. "I am so sorry. I can't imagine what you went through."

"My guilt, my dishonor, was my own doing. It was my mother who deserved better. She lost so much that day. Losing any more would destroy her. That is her greatest fear. That is why she wants me out of this fight. She would sacrifice anything for her people, for you even, but not that. Not me."

Helios' eyes, turned away throughout most of his story, snapped toward Alex with a fury born of purpose. "But I cannot fail you, Alex. Not like I did them. I will never again feel that regret. I will serve my people as my father and brother would have. I will die for them if need be. I will die for you if I must, because you are now my brother, too. I know this, instinctively, despite our limited time together. I sense a fated bond between us. Our paths are intertwined, and I will follow you as I should have followed Aureon so many years ago."

"Helios," Alex began, "I don't think that I'm... You don't owe me such loyalty. I'm no hero. Strength, wisdom, bravery... these words do not describe me. I wish I were the man you think I am, but I'm not."

Helios laughed softly. "You sound just like him. Aureon, I mean. He never knew his worth, either. In my youth, I believed it to be false modesty, just a ploy to gather praise. But he never wanted to be praised, or adored, or any other selfish thing that I thought of him. Aureon just wanted to serve. He wanted to make this realm better for the people in it. You may not believe me when I say you are much more than you think you are, but we both know you believe that this place is worth saving. I could see it on your face the moment we entered the city, and I sense that your evening about has only solidified that feeling."

"And what if I told you that I'm afraid to take this on?"

"Then I would tell you, brother, that bravery is not the absence of fear, but the willingness to act despite the fear. Were you not afraid when that root pulled you back toward the woods?"

"I was terrified," Alex responded.

"And yet, you told Lucy to let you go. Why?"

"Because I couldn't let her get dragged in with me."

Helios's eyes met Alex's once again. "Alex, I have been on countless patrols. I have fought off monsters from the Whispering Wood that still haunt my nightmares. I have fought side-by-side with some truly impressive warriors. And that moment," the Captain pounded a fist into his open palm for emphasis, "the decision you made in that moment was one of the bravest things I've ever witnessed."

A small grin bloomed on Alex's face. "I was just trying to impress Lucy."

Helios grinned back, though he tried to fight it. "Joke all you want, Alex, but you know I'm right. Deep down, you must know."

Alex thought back to that moment, the horror still fresh in his mind. The root tightening around his ankles, pulling him back into the malevolent forest. He remembered Lucy's face, the fear in her eyes. He remembered the moment of serenity when he made the decision that he would rather die alone than drag Lucy with him.

I can't lose another... The words haunted him, for some reason. It felt important, but he couldn't quite figure out why.

"So I might have..."

"No might, Alex. No maybe. You were thrust into this fight, and you have risen to the occasion multiple times. You have already proven your worth to everyone else. Why can't you see it in yourself?"

Alex remained silent. He had no answer to offer.

Helios stood, his eyes locked on Alex's. "Please, consider what I've said. Your choice is your own, but..."

"My choice is already made, Helios," Alex interrupted. "If I left this city to its fate... If I left you to deal with this alone... I don't think I could live with myself. I have my share of regrets too, but this can't be one of them. There's too much at stake."

Helios grinned wildly. "I knew you would say that, brother, because you are precisely the man you think you are not." He placed a strong hand on Alex's shoulder. "It will be an honor to prove you wrong."

Helios walked to the chamber door, then turned back. "Thank you, Alex. I wish it hadn't been necessary to disrupt your life for this, but I'm certainly glad I've had the chance to get to know you. Goodnight." With no more to say, he exited the room and closed the door quietly behind him.

Alex let out a shaking breath he hadn't realized he was holding. He could abandon these people, this place, and go back to his safe, solitary existence. Nobody would blame him for it. Nobody except himself.

This was to be the adventure he had waited his entire life for. He was probably going to die in this world, but the alternative felt worse. He could run back home, or potentially perish here fighting for people he cared about, who cared about him. It was a strange day, indeed, when death felt like the better alternative.

Bonds and Burdens

Despite the comfortable surroundings, Alex's night was anything but restful. The day's events and conversations kept playing in his mind. It was hard to believe that this journey only started the day before. He had been through so much already, his real-world life seeming like a distant memory.

As he lay in his lavish chamber, his thoughts swirled with a mixture of excitement, fear, and uncertainty. The promise he made to Helios weighed heavily on his heart. In this new world, he had found purpose, beauty, and a growing bond with the people he had met here. Yet, there was also the persistent desire to find a way back home, back to the safety and security of the life he had known, no matter how unremarkable it may have seemed.

Turning onto his side, Alex stared at the dancing silhouettes on the walls, his mind drifting back to Lucy. She was a whirlwind of contradictions. Fiercely independent, yet burdened by her past. She was a force of nature, and a woman who had captured his heart without even realizing it. Their dance in Sonata Square had been a pivotal moment, one filled with tension, affection, and unspoken understanding, but it had also been marred by his unbelievable mistake. He couldn't forget the look on her face when she pulled away, a mixture of surprise, confusion, and uncertainty.

Alex sighed and ran a hand through his hair. The desire to clear the air between them gnawed at him. He needed to find a way to apologize, to make her understand that he could suppress his feelings for the sake of their friendship. In time, he could forget. He had to. The alternative was to lose her from his life entirely, and that was just not an option. And then there was the bigger question that loomed above them all; the looming threat of the blight and their mission to confront it.

Resolute, Alex decided that tomorrow, as they prepared to enter the Conflux chamber, he would find the right moment to speak with Lucy and attempt to mend the crack in their relationship. It was not only a matter of facing their destiny, but also a matter of facing his own emotions. With that thought in mind, he closed his eyes and let the weight of the day's events pull him into a restless slumber, knowing that whatever the future held, it would be a journey of both challenge and discovery.

***

Alex jumped awake at the sound of knocking on his door. The moonlight still cast long shadows on his chamber floor, marking the early morning hour. Slowly, he swung his feet off the side of the bed and rose, Whiskers still undisturbed on the pillow next to him. Another light knock sounded as he walked toward the entryway. As he opened the door he was surprised to find Lucy waiting on the other side, a silky robe, presumably supplied by the Palace itself, hanging loosely from her shoulders and cinched tightly across her body.

"Hey... um... can we..." She ran a hand through her short auburn hair nervously. "Can we talk? Please?"

Alex gave a wistful smile. "Of course. I was hoping we'd get a chance to talk."

Alex stepped back as Lucy slid through the door. He watched her take a seat on the edge of his bed before carefully closing the door and crossing the room to sit with her. After several long moments of silence, Lucy gestured toward the sheets strewn across the bed. "Hard time sleeping?"

Alex nodded. "Yeah, lots to think about."

Lucy nodded in reply. "Yeah, me too."

Another moment of silence between the two, and then Alex began. "Lucy, I need you to know that I can fix this. I can push this away and be your friend. You're the first person who's ever really seen me. I need that. I need you. I know you don't want everything I want, but I'll..."

"I have feelings for you too, Alex." Lucy's voice was a whisper.

"...do anything to... Wait, what?" Alex stopped abruptly, unable to process what he had heard.

Lucy spoke again, only a bit louder, trembling with the effort to stay in control. "I... I have feelings for you, too." She looked at him then, eyes piercing into his in a wild mix of emotions. "I think I'm falling for you Alex, and it's fucking terrifying."

Her words had grown harsh, almost venomous, as if

speaking them was the worst thing she ever had to do. "I needed you to know this. You had no reason to apologize because I wanted it too, and it scared the shit out of me. It scared me because..."

The tears that had collected in her eyes began rolling down her cheeks. "Listen, I... his name was Brian. We met in college, sophomore year. At first, I hated him," she chuckled slightly, though the tears continued falling. "I thought he was just another entitled rich boy, until the day I saw him stop some frat idiot and his idiot friends from drugging a girl's drink at a party. He didn't know her, he didn't know the guy. He didn't even know anyone was watching. He just did the right thing, and didn't care what happened to him in the process."

She smiled at Alex then, bumping him a bit with her shoulder. "Sounds like someone else I know." The smile quickly faded as her story continued. "So these guys weren't happy with their fun being ruined, and they decided that Brian needed to pay for it. I decided that was a good time to pull out my pepper spray."

Alex smiled. "Of course you did."

"Well, I certainly wasn't going to just stand there and watch him get his ass kicked. So anyway, I got Brian out of there, got him to the clinic, and helped him file the police report. I spent most of the night with him, making sure he didn't have a concussion or something. We started dating soon after."

"You fell in love with him." It wasn't a question.

"Eventually, yes. We were together for two years. We

moved in together after Junior year. We talked about getting married after college, maybe even starting a family someday."

Alex felt the tension grow as Lucy took a deep breath, preparing to tell the part of the story she seemed to be most dreading. "But the frat jackasses had long memories. They came after us several times after that, but never anything too concerning. Then one day, Brian and I went for a hike in the mountains near the campus, and apparently they decided to follow. Three of them jumped us in a small clearing by a cliff edge. Two of them held me back and made me watch while the ring leader beat the shit out of Brian.

But he didn't count on Brian fighting back. He didn't count on Brian fighting to get to me. The whole thing got out of hand. The next thing I knew, Brian's foot slipped over the edge, then the rest of him. The assholes panicked and ran like the fucking cowards they were. I got to the edge of the cliff in time to catch Brian's hand, but I couldn't pull him up. I held on, yelling for help, but I was sliding toward the edge too." Her eyes flooded with renewed tears, her voice cracking with the grief she couldn't shake. "Then he... he told me... to let go. I didn't want to, but I... I couldn't... I had to..."

Lucy buried her face in her hands, her sobs still audible through her fingers. Instinctively, Alex pulled her to his chest, holding her tightly and stroking her hair. He said nothing. There was nothing he could say to ease this kind of pain. He simply held her close and waited until her sobs began to soften, then stop altogether.

I can't lose another... Alex's eyes widened at the realization that struck him. "Shit." He pulled away and took her hands in his. "The woods... that moment... I'm so sorry Lucy. I am so, so sorry."

Gathering herself, Lucy laid two fingers against his lips. "There's no way you could have known, Alex. Even if you had, would you have done anything differently?"

Alex shook his head slowly. "No, I guess I wouldn't."

"Of course you wouldn't, Alex. It's who you are. It's one of the reasons I..." Lucy sighed heavily. "But now you see why I can't go there again. It would destroy me."

Alex lowered his eyes from hers, any hope he had previously felt once again slipping away. "I... I understand."

"I'm sorry Alex, really I..."

"No, no apologies. I get it, Lucy. Trust me, I know all about protecting your heart. Just having you in my life is enough."

Lucy cocked her head a bit. "Is it?"

Alex shrugged. "It has to be, right? Not having you around would be so much worse."

"I feel the same." Lucy smiled, still wistful, but also tinged by a hint of relief. "Thank you for understanding, Alex." She stood then, her hands dropping away from his. "I've taken up enough of your night. Get some sleep, and I'll see you in the morning."

Alex nodded. "You too Lucy. Goodnight."

"Goodnight Alex." Lucy moved toward the chamber door, stopping with the handle half-turned. Without looking back, she said quietly, "I wish things could be different, Alex. I really do." She slipped out the door without waiting for a reply, leaving Alex alone with his thoughts once again.

Thirteen

A Mother's Touch

The dining hall was silent, save for the clinking of silverware on porcelain. Alex and Lucy had been summoned to join the royal family for breakfast before descending into the underground lair of the Lumigenesis Conflux. Lucy kept her eyes on her plate, as if looking anywhere else may betray the emotions of the early morning discussion. Helios was also unusually reserved, exchanging only occasional pleasantries with his Mother and Alex.

As the last of the food was consumed, Celestia scanned the three faces before her with a bemused expression. "Are we... ready to proceed?"

Everyone nodded in affirmation, Helios offering quietly, "Yes, Mother."

"Lios, could you please escort Lucy ahead? I would like to have a word with Alex. We shall be along shortly."

"Of course, Mother," Helios replied, standing slowly and beckoning Lucy to follow.

The Queen waited for Helios and Lucy to disappear through the door, then spoke softly. "Alex, I could not help but notice some tension between you and Lucy, and Lios is not acting himself either. Is there something I should know?"

Alex sighed, then responded, "Things with Lucy are, well, complicated. But we're working through it."

"Oh dear, you told her how you felt? And she did not reciprocate?"

"What do you mean?" Alex said, attempting to feign ignorance.

"Come now, Alex. Don't be coy," the Queen replied, repressing a laugh. "You are not very good at it. Everyone here knew how you felt about her from the moment you looked at her." She then waved a hand toward the door. "Well, except for her, of course."

Alex felt the heat creep into his cheeks as Celestia's grin widened. Finally, he yielded, "It's a long story, and much of it isn't mine to tell. We'll work through it. Our friendship is too important not to."

"I have no doubt, Alex. But I would not lose hope if I were you. I have seen how she looks at you, too."

Alex nodded silently for a moment, before looking back toward Celestia. "Queen Celestia, I had wanted to take a moment to speak with you as well. To offer my condolences for what you have lost. Who you have lost. I can't imagine..."

"He told you?" Celestia's face instantly transformed from amusement to shock, her wide eyes intently focused on Alex.

"I... I'm sorry... Was I not supposed to know? I apologize for..." Alex stumbled for words.

Celestia waved away his apologies as she regained her

composure. "No, Alex. Do not worry. I apologize for my reaction. It was not anger, merely surprise. Lios is a very private person, especially about this. For him to open up about it..." She trailed off, her expression akin to admiration as she looked into Alex's eyes. "He must have a great deal of respect for you."

Alex smiled back at the Queen. "I think Helios offers more respect than I've earned. He is a good man. I just wish he could forgive himself."

"As do I. Unfortunately, the only difference between youthful foolishness and lifelong regret is often simply fate's timing."

"Yes, I suppose so." Alex nodded. "My father passed as well, a few years back. We had been estranged since I left home. He was neglectful, abusive, sometimes violent. I was happy when I heard of his death, and it made me wonder what kind of person that made me."

Celestia's voice was soothing as she spoke. "It made you hurt, Alex. Nothing more."

"I understand that now, but it took some time to come to grips with it. I had heard that he wanted to reconnect, but I refused. After his death, I sometimes wondered if it would have made a difference."

"We all have moments in our past that we wonder if we could have changed. You must remember that you made the best decision you could at the time. Perhaps he changed, perhaps he did not, but the culmination of your decisions has made you the man seated before me. I cannot determine if you were right or wrong, but I see a strength in you that may not have come to pass if you had chosen differently."

"Thank you, Celestia. For the sake of you and your people, I hope I can live up to the man you believe me to be."

The Queen beamed back at him. "I see it now," she mused. Marking the confusion on Alex's face, she continued. " I see why Lios was able to open up with you. There was only one other that he ever felt truly comfortable confiding in." Her eyes glistened slightly, but the wide smile remained. "You remind me so much of my Auri."

Alex looked into Celestia's eyes and smiled. "I take that as a great compliment. I would..." Alex hesitated, unsure if it was appropriate to ask. "I would like to know more about Aureon one day, if it isn't too painful to talk about him."

"I would love to tell you everything, Alex. It's been so long since I've been able to... but unfortunately, we don't have the time now. I'm sure Lios and Lucy are wondering where we are."

"Of course," Alex replied, "we should probably go then."

Alex escorted Celestia through the halls leading to a massive stone stairwell, which opened to a cavernous expanse below the Palace. As Alex descended into the heart of the Lumigenesis Conflux, he was met with a sight that left him in awe. The chamber was a breathtaking blend of natural wonder and architectural grandeur. Tall, illuminated crystals adorned the walls, casting a soft, ethereal glow over the space. The air was cool and crisp, filled with a subtle, invigorating energy that seemed to hum with ancient power.

The corruption of the blight was a creeping, insidious force. Black tendrils spread from the walls toward the pool in the center, causing a subtle distortion of the room's natural luminance where they took hold. The luminescent crystals in those places, once vibrant and radiant like the rest, now flickered erratically, casting eerie, shifting shadows throughout the chamber. The corruption moved like a creeping fog, obscuring the details and veiling the room in an unsettling darkness.

As the blight's corruption advanced, the chamber's pillars and arches started to crumble and deteriorate nearby, their once-majestic carvings and symbols eroded by the malevolent force. The sounds of cracking stone and crumbling mortar filled the air, creating an eerie symphony of decay.

In the center of the chamber lay a massive, crystal-clear pool, its surface so smooth it resembled liquid glass. Shimmering prisms of light danced within the water, obscured only by the clouding of the water's edge from the blight's proximity. Intricate patterns of pure light spiraled out from a central point. This was the Conflux Pool, the source of Luterre's magic, and it pulsed with a serene, rhythmic luminescence.

Around the pool were several ornate stone platforms, each featuring unique carvings and designs that told the history of Luterre. Intricate tapestries hung from the ceiling, depicting the legends of their realm. Incense burners released fragrant, calming scents into the air. The chamber exuded a sense of ancient wisdom and mysticism.

As Alex moved closer, his eyes were drawn to a particularly vibrant tapestry hanging directly over the pool. "That can't be... can it?"

The tapestry was woven in metallic threads of various colors. In the center stood two pale-skinned figures, a man and a woman bathed in radiant light, their eyes filled with determination and strength. The man held a glowing staff, while the woman wielded a shimmering blade, both imbued with an aura of power.

Around the figures, the tapestry told the story of their journey. It showed the pair braving the perils of the Whispering Wood, confronting mythical creatures, and forging alliances with Lumoran warriors and artisans alike. The sky above them was filled with celestial symbols, representing the otherworldly favor they had gained during their quest.

The final frame foretold a climactic battle against the blight. A monstrous, dark entity loomed heavily, its malevolent presence portrayed with striking detail. The dark forces of the blight clashed with the light of Luterre, and at the center of this cosmic struggle were the two heroes, united in purpose and valor.

"Yeah, I had the same reaction," Lucy said from nearby. "Apparently, we got the abridged version of the prophecy."

"I assure you, there was no ill intent." Celestia's voice rang out as she entered behind Alex. "There was simply too much to discuss for just one meal."

Lucy nodded, looking satisfied with the response. Gesturing around the chamber, she mused, "So this is the heart of the Palace?"

Helios stepped forward. "This is the heart of the realm. This is where our world was born." He spoke with a quiet reverence, as if referring to a deity rather than a pool of water.

The energy of the Conflux Pool thrummed in response to their approach like it had been waiting for them. Perhaps it had been, if it were truly cognizant, as the Queen suggested.

The still, mirrored surface of the water began churning more and more with every step closer. By the time they reached the water's edge, they faced a torrential whirlpool, funneling upward in the center to create what looked like a doorway.

Alex looked over his shoulder, into the concerned faces of Helios and Celestia. "I'm guessing this isn't normal?"

Celestia shook her head in awe, while Helios only offered, "I have never seen this before."

Lucy looked back as well. "Should we be worried?"

The Queen, still in shock from the sight, managed to respond just above a whisper. "I... I do not know."

Lucy flashed a small grin at Alex. "Well, that's reassuring."

Alex shrugged back at her. "We've come this far." Alex then took the final step into the pool.

Alex was engulfed in the clear water of the Conflux Pool. It forced its way into his mouth, his lungs, yet the burning sensation of drowning didn't come. There was no need for breath within the Lumigenesis Conflux. It was the beginning and the end. It was everything and nothing. The small pool had become an expansive ocean of light and sound, no walls or surface in sight. He was adrift, but he was not alone.

He could sense the Conflux looming as if a protective Mother. He could feel her embrace, though he saw nothing around him but endless clear water. The bounds of his vision were murky, likely an effect of the blight trying to fight through, but the Conflux held it at bay. He then realized that Lucy was not with him.

As if reading his thoughts, a beautiful, Motherly voice entered his mind. *Lucy is on a similar journey, but you walk different paths. You are a man who inspires, who loves. You are a man of intelligence, generosity, and strength of character. However, you lack the confidence to freely explore these traits. Lucy is a woman who perseveres, who acts. She is a woman of wit, determination, and strength of will. Yet, she has closed herself off from the world. You both have very different lessons to learn.*

Who are you? Alex thought, attempting to communicate back to the disembodied voice.

I am the Mother to all. This land, its people, are mine to serve and nurture, for I gave them life. Now, my own life is threatened by an outside force of destruction. It has taken much of my creation, many of my children, and now it wishes to take me too. I am in need of your assistance if I am to survive.

I want to help, truly I do, Alex responded silently, *but I am no warrior. I can't be the one you put your faith in.*

You must have faith in yourself, as I do. As your companions do. As Lucy does. You have the heart and mind of a warrior, Alex Porter. You and Nexxus are one being. I cannot offer much, as I have little left to give, but I trust you already know how to wield this?

A beam of pure, white light flashed in front of Alex, leaving in its wake a brilliant oak staff, polished to gleaming. The runes etched along its length pulsed with blue light as if a living thing. It was the twin to the staff Nexxus carried in PixelQuest. The lights flared as his fingers touched the smooth wood, settling into a rhythm that matched his heartbeat.

You are never alone, Alex Porter. I will be part of you, in some small way, through the power of the Prisma Staff. But I am not the only one who will stand with you. Trust those who look to you, but more importantly, trust yourself.

The staff began folding in on itself, eventually contracting into balls of light in his palms. The light absorbed into his hand, spreading until Alex, himself, became the light. It continued to burn brighter until the burning blue light engulfed his vision. There was nothing left but light. No sights or sounds. The Mother was gone. Just blue, burning emptiness.

Alex awoke on the cold stone floor, sputtering and coughing as water burned in his lungs. Helios leaned over him, his voice raspy, as if he had been yelling.

"Alex! Thank Lumos. We had no idea what happened to you. We were afraid the blight had taken you."

Alex blinked, trying to focus his blurred vision. The pain in his chest made it difficult to speak. "Lu... Lucy?"

"I called Aurora in to help. She's with Lucy now."

He looked to his side, finding Lucy in a similar condition, dripping with the Conflux Pool's water. Aurora knelt beside her, helping her to sit up.

"She's okay, Alex," the Lieutenant said softly, "or at least she will be."

"Don't try to speak just yet, brother. Take your time." There was a hint of fear in Helios' eyes that made Alex's heart break for him. Brother. Helios had lost a brother once, and he acted as if he had been terrified that he would lose another.

Alex clasped Helios' hand tightly, wrapping his free arm around the Captain to pull him closer. "I'm... still here... brother."

Helios pulled back a bit, revealing a wide grin. "I should have known it would take more than a little water to keep you down." He helped Alex slowly to his feet, pulling an arm around his shoulders to keep him from falling again.

Alex looked around the room and his eyes went wide. "No, no, no! She gave... she gave too much!" Alex panicked, turning as much as Helios would allow to take in the chamber. The black tendrils of the blight had grown thicker, extending nearly to the edge of the pool. The crystals, once bright and warm, had dulled to near twilight.

"Alex, what are you talking about? Who gave too much of what?" Helios asked, perplexed.

Alex gasped for breath, still recovering from the near drowning. "The Mother! She said she... she would help, but... she gave too much. This will kill her!"

The room went silent, all eyes fixated on Alex, then Lucy, then back again.

Celestia stepped toward Alex. "The Mother?" She didn't even try to hide the disbelief in her voice. "You spoke with the Mother? Not a soul in recorded history has ever heard the Mother's voice." She then turned to Lucy. "And you as well?"

Lucy, finally standing with Aurora's assistance, nodded in affirmation.

"Great Lumos," Helios whispered. "Incredible."

"Did she?" Lucy caught Alex's eyes with her own, then gestured weakly to his hands.

Alex nodded, then extended his arm, fingers outstretched. A tremor of light traveled down his arm and gathered in his palm before flashing a brilliant white. As the glow faded, it revealed the staff now clenched in his fist.

Lucy smiled, taking a step away from Aurora before extending both hands out, a similar light extending to her palms as well, then flashing to reveal two wicked-looking curved blades.

"That is not possible!" Celestia's voice was quiet. The shock in her eyes was unmistakable as she took in the scene. "The Prisma Staff? The Starfall Sabers? These weapons have been lost for... for centuries! There is not even mention of them in our histories, save for the ancient archives." Her shock gradually gave way to elation, a smile spreading across her face. "Do you see now that you are, indeed, the heroes we have been waiting for?"

Alex looked at Lucy, taking in the blades she now carried. Brightly polished steel met gleaming bronze at the cross guard. Within her grip was a leather-wrapped pommel, a jeweled hilt at the end. The short swords were as beautiful as they were deadly. *Interesting that the weapon matches the wielder so well, Alex mused to himself.*

Isn't it, though? Lucy's voice said in his mind.

The two looked at each other in stunned silence.

"Did you just..." Lucy stammered.

"Yeah, I did." Alex nodded incredulously.

"What the hell happened to us in there?" Lucy turned to Celestia. "Why can I hear his thoughts?"

The Queen put a finger to her lips pensively. "Interesting. I cannot be certain, but the Mother's power now resides in both of you. Perhaps bonding with her formed a link between you and Alex, as well."

"It's as good a theory as any." Helios shrugged. "I believe we've already established that this has far surpassed the depth of our knowledge. To truly understand any of this would require a team of scholars and the entirety of the ancient archives."

"There will be a time to find answers," Celestia proclaimed, "but for now, I think we have had enough excitement for one morning. Lucy, Alex, I am sure you would like to get out of those wet clothes and rest after your visit with the Mother. Shall we reconvene this afternoon?"

"Of course. Thank you, Queen Celestia." Alex gave a small bow as the staff flashed again, the light swallowed back into his palm.

Lucy looked around the chamber, her own weapons fading back into her body as well. Surrounded by the new damage caused by the Mother's sacrifice, she whispered to the darkness, "We will not allow this gift to be wasted, if we can help it."

Fourteen

Embracing the Light

Alex walked through the dim halls of the Palace, passing by the dark corners and crumbling pillars of the quickly progressing blight. The carvings and paintings all around him had taken on a tarnish that made his stomach turn. Along the way, he reflected on his conversation with the Mother, and the sacrifice she had made to help them. The Mother had put her faith in him. He could only hope that her faith was not misplaced.

Are you on your way? Lucy's voice entered his mind, jarring him from his contemplation.

I'm almost there. I don't think this will ever not be weird, by the way.

But it's fun though, especially when I can feel that I scared you. Alex could sense her laughing at him.

You didn't scare me, Alex responded defensively. *I just wasn't expecting it.*

Right, Nexxus doesn't get scared. Alex could feel the sarcasm dripping from those words. *Hurry up, before Helios gathers the search party.*

Alex passed through the door to the throne room, immediately turning to find Lucy grinning. "You know, I don't think the Mother gave us this ability so you can mock me from afar."

Lucy let out a laugh, a ringing, sweet sound that threatened to cause Alex's knees to buckle. "Oh, Alex. Lighten up. Now we can get to know each other better than we ever thought possible."

Celestia turned to Helios, who had been watching the show with great amusement. "I believe our friends here have been practicing without us, Lios."

"It would seem so, Mother. An unorthodox training tactic, to say the least." Helios' grin widened at the scowl Alex sent in his direction. "Alright, fun aside. The Mother's sacrifice has accelerated our time frame considerably. We need a plan, and we need to find out what those weapons can do."

Alex looked to Helios. "I believe we may be covered on one of those fronts. The Mother chose my weapon because it is identical to the staff Nexxus carries. She implied that it had the same properties, as well."

"The same is true of my blades," Lucy added. "She mentioned that I already know how to wield them."

Helios cocked an eyebrow. "Care to demonstrate?"

"Probably best not to do it in here, Captain," Alex replied. "The palace has been through enough."

Helios' face paled slightly. "That powerful?"

"These weapons draw power from the wielder. The

stronger the wielder, the stronger the weapon." Alex shrugged. "If I'm right about all this, these weapons, theoretically, have infinite power."

Queen Celestia stepped forward. "I see now why they were hidden away so many years ago. That much power could be devastating in the wrong hands." Celestia looked at her two young champions with pride. "Thankfully, you both show great wisdom and strength of character, and that is why the Mother chose you."

Alex felt the weight of her words and the gravity of their situation. "We'll try not to let you down, Queen Celestia. We'll do everything we can to restore Lumora, our world, and the Conflux."

"Good," Helios chimed in. "Now, about our plan. With your new abilities, it's clear you can communicate across distances. We should work on refining that ability for tactical communication during our mission. Also, we'll need to train and understand the full capabilities of your new weapons. I think we should begin with basic weapons training before we begin sparring sessions to see how they perform in action."

Lucy raised an eyebrow. "And I suppose you're the one to train us?"

Helios grinned. "Well, I am Captain of the Guard. It is technically within my purview. I'll bring Aurora in to assist, but I have a feeling you two will be quick studies, considering everything you've already faced."

Alex glanced around the tarnished and fading grandeur of the throne room. "We should also think about the palace's defense. It's not just the Conflux that's at risk. The blight is coming, and we need to prepare for any potential assault."

Queen Celestia nodded in agreement. "Excellent point, Alex. We must gather our most skilled warriors to defend the palace. We must do all we can to hold back the blight and protect the Conflux."

"I've already begun preparations, Mother," Helios said. "We have gathered contingents of guards and Lumarchs along the perimeter to slow the spread."

Alex looked perplexedly at Helios. "Lumarchs?"

"Light wielders. Something akin to priests in your world," Helios explained. "They are gifted people who are more attuned to the Mother's light than others. Their primary job is to maintain the Conflux, but they are also tasked with magical support for the Lumoran guard."

"We still have a lot to learn about this place," Lucy mused. "Will they be able to help us fight?"

Celestia shook her head solemnly. "I am afraid not. Lumarchs do not hold nearly the power it would take to be of any use to you. Some are gifted healers, however. Perhaps…"

"Kaleigh," Helios interrupted. "We are heading into the fight of our lives. Kaleigh is the only healer I would trust at our backs. She is not only a gifted Lumarch healer, but she is one of the few who has accepted the offer of weapons training, and she is progressing well."

"It is settled then." The Queen nodded before turning to the door. "Lysander."

As if summoned from the ether, Lysander appeared within the doorway. "Yes, your Majesty?"

"Would you please send word to Kaleigh Britewaith? I would like her to join us for this meeting."

"Of course, your Majesty." Lysander bowed deeply. "I will

send a courier immediately." With that, he was off, exiting as fast as he had appeared.

Alex grinned at Helios. "You were right. He is quick for an old guy."

"I heard that too, Mr. Porter." Lysander's voice echoed from the foyer.

Helios' throaty laugh filled the throne room as the group waited for their new member to arrive.

A short time later, Lysander reappeared in the doorway. "Ms. Britewaith has arrived, your Majesty."

"Thank you, Lysander. Please send her in."

Lysander bowed, then turned wordlessly and left.

Celestia sighed. "We have been friends since we were children, and I still have yet to pull the stick from that man's…"

"Mother!" Helios admonished.

The conversation came to an abrupt halt as a young woman stepped through the door. She was hunched slightly, her hands fiddling nervously with the clasps on her cobalt tunic. Her down-turned eyes showed hints of silver amid the crystal blue. She stopped abruptly as she looked up to find four pairs of eyes watching her intently, dropping immediately to one knee in reverence.

"Have I done something wrong, your Highness?" Her voice trembled as she spoke.

"No, of course not, my dear. Please stand," Celestia said in a calm, soothing voice. "Come in, Kaleigh. We have need of your expertise."

Kaleigh rose to her feet, far more relaxed than she had been moments earlier. "Of course, my queen."

Helios stepped forward, clasping Kaleigh's hand in

greeting. "Thank you for joining us. I have requested you, specifically, because of your training in both light-wielding and combat. You are uniquely qualified to aid our quest."

"I am honored to serve, Captain."

Helios held up a hand to stop her. "Before you agree to this, you must know the stakes. I would never force you to take on such responsibility, especially at such risk."

Helios started by introducing Alex and Lucy, before moving on to his explanation. As Helios spoke, relaying recent events and the plans that lay ahead, Kaleigh's face paled. The nervous fidgeting returned as she listened, her fingers trailing along the seams of her tunic from one clasp to the next. By the time Helios had finished, Kaleigh had the look of a woman who was readying herself to flee.

"As I said, Kaleigh, this is not an order," Helios finished. "Each of us has chosen this path. If you choose to join us, it will be of your own volition, and fully understanding the risks involved."

"Captain, if I may ask, why me?" Kaleigh's voice was soft, almost childlike, edged by fear and doubt.

"You are a talented light-wielder Kaleigh, but I have also watched you progress quickly in the training ring. We will need someone of your talent to complete this mission, and I believe you are the only one of the Lumarchs with the fighting skills to match."

Kaleigh nodded absently. "Understood." She took a deep breath to steady herself, her delicate hands smoothing down the front of her tunic before finally resting at her sides. Suddenly, her eyes shifted, fear giving way to a fiery determination that looked far too old for such a young face. "You are aware that my mother is an elder in the Lumarch community, correct?"

Celestia moved forward to face the young Lumarch. "Your mother is much more than that Kaleigh. Valia Britewaith is the most powerful light-wielder we have seen in decades."

Kaleigh nodded with pride. "When I was a child, she once told me that she heard whispers from the Mother. She said that the Mother had plans for me. I believe this is what she was talking about. I have devoted my life in service to the Mother and this city. I cannot refuse when she needs me most. You have my light and my sword. I will do what I can."

Alex offered his hand in gratitude. "Thank you for joining us, Kaleigh. We need all the help we can get."

Kaleigh took his hand, giving it a gentle shake. "This is my home. It is I who should be thanking you." Turning toward Lucy, she added, "Both of you."

Lucy grinned. "You're saving me from being outnumbered on the road. No thanks required."

Kaleigh laughed, an uninhibited melody that often accompanied youth. Alex would have guessed her to be no more than sixteen, if it weren't for her eyes. Silver-rimmed and full of wisdom, her eyes were a blue that Alex hadn't thought possible, crystalline to the point of nearly being clear. Kaleigh's eyes reminded him of the pool below the palace, before the blight had marred it, somehow both youthful and ageless.

Alex didn't want to imagine those eyes losing their luster, fading as the Conflux pool had. Realizing the possibilities of what lay ahead, he prayed to the Mother that he wouldn't have to see it happen.

Fifteen

Magic and Mastery

Alex stood in the center of the training ring, the Prisma Staff thrumming in his hands. His breath was labored, sweat dripping from his forehead. They had been working with training staves for hours already, as they had for the three days prior. This time, however, Helios had finally decided that Alex was ready for the real thing.

"Where's Lucy?" Alex looked around the ring, but she was nowhere to be found.

"Don't worry about Lucy. She's with Lieutenant Artisynth. Blade training," Helios responded. "Now focus. Are you ready for this?"

Alex took a deep breath, then nodded. "Let's do it."

Alex took a fighting stance, left foot forward, holding the staff angled before him as Helios had taught him. He thought back to his considerable experience as Nexxus, envisioning the movements his character had made thousands of times before. Giving another slight nod, Alex took a wide step with his back foot, allowing his hips to follow through as his right hand swept forward, then up. The bottom of the staff came forward in a wide arc, snapping to a stop as it trained on the target.

Nothing happened. The only indication of the staff's power was the constant pulsing of blue light, beating in time with Alex's heart.

"Did…" Alex began breathlessly. "Did I do it wrong?"

Helios put a hand on his shoulder. "I'm sure it just takes practice. Try again."

Alex regained his stance, reviewing the movements once again in his mind. Another deep breath. Another arcing attack. Still nothing.

Kaleigh, who had been watching eagerly from the edge of the ring, approached Alex. She stopped just before him, gently placing a hand on his arm. "Alex, you're coming at this like a warrior. You're too focused on the movements of the attack. Light-wielding is about connecting with the land, the Mother. Let me ask you this; when you summon the staff, what are you thinking about?"

Alex considered for a moment. "I'm not really thinking about anything. I just do it."

"Exactly!" Kaleigh pointed a slender finger into his chest. "It comes from here," she then lifted her hand, her finger resting on his temple, "not here. You are Guardian, but you are also Lumarch. You must learn to combine the two."

Alex nodded, retaking his stance once again as Kaleigh stepped away.

"Your body knows what to do, Alex," Kaleigh spoke

softly. "Connect with the Mother. She'll guide you the rest of the way."

Alex took another deep breath, sparing a glance around the ring. The training area had been cleared for this session to avoid bystanders in the line of fire, but none had left the courtyard. Hopeful faces surrounded the perimeter, eager to catch a glimpse of the legendary weapon and the hero who wielded it.

"No pressure, right?" Alex mumbled to himself, closing his eyes. *Mother, I want to serve you, but I need your help.* His silent words awakened something in him. A warmth, deep inside his chest, began to spread throughout his body, down his arms, into his hands. It connected with the staff. No, he connected with the staff, its essence merging with his as if the staff was an extension of his body.

His eyes opened, barely catching the startled expression on Kaleigh's face in his periphery as he set his sights on the target. He was only vaguely aware of his body as it swept effortlessly through the motions he had been practicing. The runes of the staff flared brightly as it came forward, drawing with it an arc of blue flame that traveled forward at an inexplicable speed. The pile of hay bales that had been set out as a target erupted in those blue flames, falling away to nothing but ash almost instantly.

The training area, teeming moments ago with excitement and anticipation, went completely silent. More than a hundred guards stood in shock at the power they had just witnessed. As the flames died down and the power of the staff quieted, the only sound remaining was Alex's ragged breathing.

Alex stood frozen in his finishing stance, his heart racing as if it would fly out of his chest. The rush of power had been exhilarating, but its sudden absence left him drained. The HUD that had become common in his vision appeared once again, the mana bar draining almost completely. He stood a moment longer before cheers erupted from all around him. He looked around at the hopeful faces surrounding the edge of the training ring, turning finally to face Helios and Kaleigh, beaming with pride.

The smiles faded quickly, however, as Kaleigh approached, wide-eyed. "Your eyes..." she said, almost in a whisper. "They're still..."

"What about my eyes?" Alex asked, panicking slightly.

Kaleigh produced a small mirror from the pouch hanging from her belt. "Here, see for yourself."

Alex peered into the glass, studying his hazel eyes intently. But they were no longer simply hazel. Veins of cobalt ran through his eyes like lightning bolts, slowly fading from the intense glow of just moments ago. The glow finally receded, but the blue remained, as if he was forever marked by the power he held.

"I saw the lightning flash in your eyes, but I thought it was just the power gathering. Getting marked by the light is... well, it's extremely rare. The only living person I know of is..." Kaleigh trailed off.

"Your mother?" Alex presumed.

Kaleigh nodded. "If your light rivals hers..." The possibilities hung in the words she didn't say. Great, and terrible possibilities.

"Are you saying that this," Helios said incredulously,

gesturing toward the scorched earth where the hay bales once stood, "is not the extent of the staff's power?"

"I'm saying," Kaleigh corrected, "that this is not the extent of Alex's power, staff or no staff."

"It certainly feels like it is," Alex said, weariness tinging his voice. "That was exhausting. One attack and I have nothing left."

Kaleigh smiled, her eyes sparkling. "That's what training is for."

The trio continued their training session for several hours more, focusing mainly on light attacks and shielding. Helios stood by, correcting Alex's form when needed, while Kaleigh gave occasional tips on connecting with the Mother and focusing the light. At first, frequent breaks were needed for Alex to replenish his mana. But soon the breaks became less and less necessary, Alex's abilities becoming more efficient and, by extension, using less of his stamina as he practiced.

As the sun met the horizon, the blue skies giving way to the purples and reds of twilight, Alex stood haggard in the center of the ring. Most of the onlookers had disbursed, though a few stragglers remained, still in awe of the demonstration of power. Helios and Kaleigh stood nearby, looking very pleased with the progress Alex had made with their guidance.

"It looks like you could use a meal and rest," Helios said as he approached.

"No, I want to keep going," Alex replied breathlessly, still exhilarated from the power he felt coursing through him.

"Trust me, Alex. That's the adrenaline talking. You need to rest before you crash, and I don't want to explain to Lucy why I have to carry you inside. I've taken on bog wythes that scare me less than her when she's angry."

Alex looked quizzically at Helios. "Bog wythe?"

"You don't want to know."

Alex took a moment to take stock of his body. His muscles burned, exhausted from use. His mind raced as his focus waned. He nodded. "Yeah, maybe resting is a good idea."

As the three compatriots walked back to the palace entrance, Alex felt the intensity of the day's events rush from his body, leaving behind the soreness and exhaustion that Helios had warned of. It was a discomfort that he had never truly known before, but it was also a mark of the power, the light that he had commanded in that circle.

He thought back to the crowds around the training ring. The cacophony of cheers that had erupted after that first successful attack echoed through his mind. These people were looking to him for help. He and Lucy were their only sources of hope for their home to be restored. He didn't have the heart to tell them that he was the wrong man for the job, and it didn't seem like anyone would listen if he tried.

Sixteen

Old Connections and New Beginnings

As Alex entered his chambers to clean up before dinner, he caught sight of Whiskers curled up on the bed. "Hi, buddy. I missed you today."

Whiskers stretched in response, then looked back at Alex as he approached. Whiskers jumped to his feet, backing away from Alex as if avoiding a predator. *EYES!* he exclaimed silently.

Alex stopped abruptly. "Right, sorry. I know it's different, but it's still me. I promise." He held out a hand to his furry companion.

Whiskers approached slowly, sniffing at the air tentatively. As he got within inches of Alex's fingers, he relaxed visibly. *Still you,* he purred before sliding his head into Alex's outstretched hand.

"Yeah, buddy. Still me."

Whiskers rubbed his head against Alex's hand a few more times before circling twice, then plopping back down on the bed to continue his nap. Alex, satisfied and relieved that his furry friend still recognized him, began stripping off his sweat-soaked tunic before heading into the washroom to clean up.

A short time later, Alex walked the halls of the Palace once again. He took note of the tarnished, dingy artwork along the way. They had not gotten any worse since the day the Mother had sacrificed so much for them, but they hadn't gotten any better either. She was still fighting, but she wasn't winning. Alex said a silent thank you to the Mother for buying them time as he walked, renewing his vow to restore her to her former glory.

As Alex turned the final corner toward the dining hall, he nearly bumped into Kaleigh.

"Alex, you're looking refreshed."

Alex laughed. "It's amazing what a bit of soap and water will do. Are you joining us for dinner?"

"I am," Kaleigh replied, "if that's ok."

Alex smiled, "I mean, it's not really my decision, but I'm more than happy to have you." Kaleigh blushed slightly, causing Alex to stumble over his words as he attempted to clarify. "For dinner... I mean at dinner... I..." Alex sighed as he resolved that there was no saving himself in this situation. Instead, he simply gestured down the hall and said, "Shall we?"

Kaleigh laughed as Alex's face turned varying shades of red. "Yes, we shall."

Helios, Aurora, and Lucy had already arrived when Alex

and Kaleigh walked in. "Kaleigh, I assume you already know Lieutenant Artisynth," Alex said as they entered.

"Rori and I have known each other since we were children, though we had lost touch for a long time."

Aurora spoke up then. "Imagine my surprise when I was told that a Lumarch was joining us for training, and in walks my childhood best friend, little Kay Britewaith... well, not so little anymore." She smiled at the last, her voice holding a hint of something deeper.

Kaleigh grinned back at her. "Oh, you were always the charmer, weren't you? You haven't changed a bit. Still gorgeous, still witty, and still an insatiable flirt."

Lucy, enjoying the banter between the two, finally turned to look at Alex. Startled, she jumped to her feet, crossing the room briskly. "Alex! Your eyes!"

Alex grinned. "I've been getting that a lot lately."

"What happened?" Lucy asked, fear masking her face.

"Apparently, I've been marked, right Kaleigh?" Alex looked to find the Lumarch deeply distracted by the sight of her friend at the table. "Kaleigh?"

"Yes, sorry, what?" Kaleigh stumbled, "Oh, right, the marking. It's not dangerous, just a symbol of the Mother's power. Given that your power was acquired in the same way, you should probably be prepared to take on the mark as well."

"Oh, okay, good," Lucy sighed in relief. "Well, it actually suits you, Alex. Your eyes were already... well... this is a whole new dynamic. Kinda bad-ass, if you ask me." Lucy grinned, causing Alex to smile in return.

Alex was famished, far more so than he realized as he sat at the table. The meal consisted mainly of bread and cheeses from the market in town, though the palace was able to summon enough magic to produce a small bit of roast pork. It was a simple meal, but to Alex, it was delicious.

Queen Celestia was away for the evening with duties to attend to, so there was no real planning to be done. Instead, the group sat as friends, talking and laughing.

"So, Kaleigh." Lucy leaned in. "I have to know what Rori was like when she was younger."

"No, Kay," Aurora retorted, laughing. "Lucy does not need to know any of that. Nobody ever needs to know."

Kaleigh grinned. "So I shouldn't tell them about the time you stole an entire barrel of ale from the back door of the tavern? Or the time you lit fireworks in the market square and scared everyone half to death?"

Aurora gasped in mock indignation. "Excuse me? That was your idea."

Kaleigh laughed, then continued. "What about the time we snuck out after sunset to go dancing in Sonata Square?"

Aurora sighed. "Then we laid under the stars until dawn. That was a great night."

Kaleigh's eyes misted slightly, her smile fading. "It was the first time we... the only time..."

Aurora took Kaleigh's hand, her face somber with longing. "I am so sorry, Kay. I would have given anything for things to be different."

Kaleigh looked back at her childhood friend. "I need to ask. I'm sorry to bring this up, but I need to know... I mean, I get why you ran from your father, but why did you run from me?"

Aurora's somber face turned to one of outrage, her eyes

burning with a ferocity that would have made an ogre run in fear. "Is that what that bastard told you? That arrogant, hateful, lying piece of... He said I ran?" The indignation in her voice was palpable. She took a moment to breathe, calming slightly before she spoke again. "Kay, if I had run, it would have been to you. Your mother would have taken me in, I know that. I never would have left you if..."

Tears started rolling down her cheeks as she spoke. "That night in Sonata Square, laying under the stars... when I got home after sunrise, he was sitting at the table waiting for me. He wanted to know where I had been. I ignored him at first, but he just kept yelling, so I told him. I told him about you. I told him about us... by the end of the day, he had me shipped off. First boarding school, then guard training. He said that discipline would 'fix' me."

The room went silent. Horrified faces looked on as Aurora finished her story. Finally, tears began spilling from Kaleigh's eyes as she found her voice. Shaking her head incredulously, she sobbed softly, "Why did I ever believe... I was so hurt for so long. Rori, can you ever forgive me?"

Confused, Aurora looked up at Kaleigh. "Forgive you? For what?"

Kaleigh's eyes were trained on the floor, as if looking up at the woman in front of her would undo her somehow. "For thinking the worst of you. For believing that you had just left me behind."

Aurora crooked a finger under Kaleigh's chin, pulling her closer until their eyes met from inches apart. "You have nothing to apologize for. He was the only one left who knew what he did, and he was never going to tell you the truth. This is on him, Kaybee, not you."

Kaleigh's eyes lit up at the last, the corners of her mouth curling slightly. "You haven't called me that in a really long time. I forgot how much I missed it."

Aurora moved forward, pressing her forehead against Kaleigh's. "So did I," she said softly, closing the distance until their lips gently pressed together.

***

Alex sat in the reading nook of his chamber, the lantern flickering overhead. The growing stack of books he had already finished cast a long, dancing shadow across the floor. As he sat thumbing through another tome, he was interrupted by a soft knock on the door.

"Come in."

The latch clicked as the door swung open and Lucy slipped inside, her silken nightgown flowing from her hips like running water. She picked at her fingernails as she crossed the room, her eyes downcast.

"Is something wrong?" Alex asked nervously.

"No, there's nothing wrong. Just..." She hesitated, turning back toward the door, as if she was simply going to walk away. She stopped again, then turned back. "I'm so not good at this, but I just... you know... at dinner tonight. Listening to Rori and Kaleigh... the regret, the longing... it just got me thinking."

Alex put his book down and stood. "Thinking about what?" His heart was racing at the possibilities, and he fought to keep himself in check.

"It broke my heart to hear about the time they lost. I don't ever want to look back one day and realize... I've closed myself off to so much, Alex. I thought I had to protect my heart after... you know... after Brian. And it worked for me for a long time. I never felt like I was missing something until..."

Lucy was quiet for a long time. Alex took a step forward, narrowing the distance between them. "Lucy, please talk to me. Whatever you're trying to say, you can tell me."

Lucy took a step forward as well, moving mechanically, as if trying and failing to hold herself back. "Alex, I'm trying to tell you... I'm trying to say that..." She took a deep breath to steady herself. As resolve set in, she finally raised her chin, revealing her emerald eyes shining with unshed tears in the moonlight. "Damn it, I love you, Alex, and I want to be with you. We might never make it out of this place, might never make it through this fight, and I don't want to go another damn moment trying to convince myself that I don't need you."

Alex stood in stunned silence. He had tried so hard not to hope for this, and now that it had happened, he didn't know how to respond.

"Alex, say something, please."

The first tear trailed down Lucy's cheek in the silence, and something in Alex screamed that he could not let that tear fall to the floor. He had to act, or he would lose her forever.

The corner of Alex's lip twitched as he looked into Lucy's eyes. "No."

Lucy looked at him, confused. "No?"

Alex smiled and took the final step to her, close enough that a deep breath would press the length of their bodies together. "I have nothing to say." His left hand trailed along her waist, finally resting on the small of her back. Gently, he pulled her closer as he ran the thumb of his right hand along her cheek, his fingers sliding through her hair to the back of her neck.

Alex's eyes softened as his gaze met Lucy's. "You're sure about this?"

Lucy bit her bottom lip, looking up at him. "I'm not going anywhere this time."

He brushed his mouth lightly against hers, drawing a shaking breath from her lips. "You see what you do to me, Lucy Watts? You give me courage I didn't know I had." Before she could respond, his lips pressed against hers gently.

Their mouths moved in tandem, simply exploring at first. As the kiss grew into something more, their hunger became a living thing between them. They each fed that hunger, lips parting to delve further into each other, tasting one another in a way that they had denied for far too long. They took their time, fighting back the urgency of their needs, allowing themselves to savor every moment.

Lucy's hands ran up Alex's back, and he pressed closer to her in response. They merged together, holding each other so tightly that it felt as though their racing hearts would eventually meet.

Alex pulled back from the kiss breathlessly. "I love you too, Lucy. I've been waiting for someone like you for a long time."

Lucy smiled back at Alex, a brilliant smile that made her eyes sparkle. Between her own ragged breaths, she chuckled a bit as she said, "just remember who said it first."

Seventeen

The Weight of Destiny

Alex and Lucy walked, hand in hand, through the entry of the grand throne room, finding Celestia, Helios, and Aurora waiting for them.

"Ah, Lucy! There you are," Aurora called out. "I was looking for you earlier, but you weren't in your room." A wide grin spread across her lips as she gestured to their joined hands. "I assume you found… other accommodations last night?"

Alex's face heated at the implication. Looking at Lucy, he noticed a slight reddening of her cheeks before a sly grin spread across her face. "Are you telling me that you went home alone last night, Lieutenant Artisynth?"

This time, it was Aurora's turn to blush, a response that nobody in the room would have ever expected from the shameless flirt.

"It seems," the Queen interjected, "that I missed a great deal yesterday."

Helios laughed. "It seems that I've missed something myself. But let's be honest, we were all waiting for it to happen."

Celestia flashed a grin at her son, a sure indication that she was up to no good. "If that blush is any indication, I would bet that it 'happened' quite a bit."

"Mother! Would you please stop saying things like that in front of me?"

"Lios," the Queen chided, "if I remember correctly, we had this talk when you were younger."

"Yes, and it was mortifying then too." Helios shrank into himself as if he could disappear entirely.

Queen Celestia chuckled a bit, before her attention was drawn to the door.

Kaleigh stepped inside, stopping to take in the scene. "Sorry I'm late, your Highness." She looked from face to face, noting the Captain's discomfort, the Celestia's amusement, and the trio of blushing faces around them. "Did I... miss something?"

"Lumarch Britewaith, nice to see you again." Aurora spoke in her most official tone, though the smile she was fighting tugged at the corners of her mouth relentlessly.

Kaleigh, losing a similar fight to school her face, replied, "Lieutenant Artisynth, a pleasure as always."

Lucy looked from one woman to the other before a smirk overtook her face. "You two aren't fooling anyone. You know that, right?"

A snicker ran through the room as Kaleigh sheepishly took her place beside Aurora.

Celestia held up a hand, silencing the room. "I have asked you all to gather this morning to discuss the distressing business I was attending to yesterday. The farms in the outskirts of the city are becoming barren at an alarming rate, and livestock populations are rapidly depleting. Furthermore, the rivers and coastline are nearly saturated with blight, affecting our drinking water supplies and fisheries. I fear we are out of time. We must act swiftly if we are to save our people from suffering."

Helios sighed heavily before snapping to attention, instantly transforming into the authoritative Captain of the Guard. "I had hoped we would have more time. Lieutenant, how is Lucy's training progressing?"

"Well Captain," Aurora said, stepping forward, "her skills are progressing well, but I would be more comfortable with a few more sessions. We haven't even gotten to light-wielding yet."

Helios frowned slightly. "We have no more time, Lieutenant. Light-wielding is your new priority today. Lumarch Britewaith, please join them. Your insight was an immense help with Alex."

"Of course, Captain," Kaleigh replied with a small bow. "Thank you for your trust in me."

"Well earned, Lumarch Britewaith," Helios replied, dismissing the trio to their training.

As the three women left, Helios turned to Alex. "Brother, I am happy with the progress you've made in the ring. Under better circumstances, I would prefer to ensure your readiness for battle, but we must gather supplies for the journey ahead. I'm afraid I need you out of the training area today."

Alex nodded. "Understood. I don't know if I'm ready or not, but I guess we'll find out soon enough."

Helios turned to Celestia with a small bow. "Mother, we will make preparations and return to discuss travel plans."

The Queen bowed her head in acknowledgment, her face carefully masked to hide the concern which her eyes betrayed. "Of course, Lios. We will meet again before sundown. I would like to give everyone the evening to get affairs in order before you leave tomorrow."

Helios nodded, then turned to Alex with a forlorn look and gestured toward the door. "We should get moving," he said quietly. A slight hesitation, then he moved quickly through the door to the foyer with Alex close behind.

Alex and Helios walked in silence through the majestic halls of the palace, the atmosphere weighed down by the gravity of their impending mission. The realization that they had little time left to prepare for their journey was difficult to reconcile. The training, the preparation had all led up to this, but somewhere in the back of Alex's mind, it was never truly real.

As they passed the frayed and tattered tapestries that chronicled the kingdom's storied history, Alex couldn't help but feel a sense of unease. It was one thing to play a hero in a virtual world, but facing a real, life-threatening challenge was an entirely different matter. He couldn't shake the feeling of trepidation that gnawed at him.

Helios, too, wore a pensive expression, his thoughts seemingly a world away from the regal surroundings. He glanced at Alex, his eyes reflecting both concern and determination.

"We don't have a choice, Alex. Our people are counting on us. It's a heavy burden, but we'll face it together."

Alex nodded, grateful for the Captain's support. In this surreal, video game-like realm of Luterre, the line between reality and fantasy had blurred beyond recognition. The fate of two worlds rested on their shoulders, and it was a responsibility they couldn't evade.

They made their way to the palace's armory, a room brimming with a dazzling array of weapons, armor, and supplies. Helios took charge, swiftly assessing their needs and instructing Alex on what to gather. "We'll need provisions for the journey and rations to last us through unknown territories. Grab some water flasks, first aid supplies, and anything else you think might be useful. Once travel preparations are complete, we will choose your armor."

Alex looked at the Captain with concern. "I haven't trained in armor. Won't that make it hard for me to fight?"

"We will find you something light and well formed. You will sacrifice some level of protection, but your mobility will be preserved." Alex attempted to protest, but Helios cut him off. "Please, brother. I know you have the ability to shield, but I would feel better if you had an extra layer of protection. If your light falters at the wrong moment…"

There was a pain in Helios' eyes that Alex couldn't bring himself to argue with. He nodded in surrender. "Okay, I'll give it a shot."

Alex followed the instructions he was given, his movements mechanical as he collected items and stuffed them into satchels. Every step felt like a countdown to an unknown destiny, and the weight of their mission pressed heavily on his chest.

As they continued to prepare, Alex wondered about Lucy and Kaleigh's progress. He hoped they were making headway, as their abilities would undoubtedly be crucial in confronting the blight that plagued the kingdom.

Helios, as if sensing his thoughts, looked up from his own preparations. "Don't worry about Lucy and Kaleigh. They're strong and capable. They'll catch up quickly."

The Captain's words brought a glimmer of reassurance to Alex. He had to be sure that Lucy was ready for this; that she could protect herself. It wasn't about strength, of course. Lucy had more than enough of that. But they had no idea what they would end up facing, and Alex couldn't bear the thought of anything happening to her.

Their satchels packed and ready, Helios handed Alex a vest of thick leather, small shingles reminiscent of dragon scales adorning much of the lower torso. The lion crest of Lumora was carved into the chest, and the back was affixed with leather straps and buckles. "Try this."

Alex slid his arms through the openings, allowing Helios to tighten straps and buckles until the armor was secured around him like a second skin.

Helios handed him a training staff from a nearby rack. "Go through a few motions. See how it feels."

Alex attempted a few strikes and parries, his movements stiff and blocky. "This isn't going to work. I can't turn my body."

Helios made a few adjustments to the straps along his ribs. "That should help. Try now."

Once again, Alex practiced striking and parrying, finishing in a large sweeping motion. "Better. It will take some getting used to, but I can work with this."

Satisfied, Helios then handed Alex a pair of leather bracers, simply designed with three buckles to hold them in place on his forearms. "And these?"

Alex tried the bracers on as well, once again testing his form. Finally, he nodded. "Again, it will take some time, but these will work."

Helios looked at Alex for a moment, then pulled a dagger and sheath from his belt. The handle of etched ivory bore symbols that he recognized from the Conflux chamber. The exposed section of the polished blade gleamed brightly in the dimness of the armory, as if creating its own light. "This belonged to Aureon. I want you to carry it with you."

Alex shook his head vehemently. "No Helios, I can't..."

"You can, and you must, Alex. If he were here, he would most certainly be by your side. Now, in some small way, he will be."

Alex hesitated momentarily before reaching his hand out. "Thank you, brother. I will try to live up to this honor."

"I have no doubt that you will, Alex. It's who you are."

Alex tucked the dagger firmly into his belt before gathering two of the satchels and his new armor. Helios slung the remaining supplies over his shoulder and, together, they moved on to finish preparations.

The sun hung just above the tree line by the time they had finished. Returning to the Palace, they made their way to a small meeting room where the Queen awaited them, along with Lucy, Aurora, and Kaleigh.

The mood was somber as they entered, the gravity of the next morning like a low-hanging fog in the room. Lucy stood and approached when she saw Alex in the doorway, pressing a gentle kiss to his lips. Alex looked into her green eyes, newly marked with blue lightning spidering from her pupils. "You couldn't just let me have this one, could you?"

Lucy laughed, despite the melancholy of the room. "Come on Alex. You know I can't just let you win. That wouldn't be any fun."

Alex savored that laugh, letting it encase him in the small joy of the moment. He then looked from face to face, everyone's eyes reflecting the weight of their mission and the uncertainty of what lay ahead. Sighing heavily, he pressed his forehead against Lucy's. "We should probably get to it then."

As the discussions began, maps were spread across the table, plans were made, and strategies were outlined. Planning for something like this was difficult, as they had no real idea what they would be facing, or even looking for.

Their search would begin near the Whispering Wood, just east of the failing Binaural Divide, the barrier between the human world and Luterre. It was likely that the Divide's fall was an indication of the blight source's proximity. The fate of Luterre, and also the human world, hinged on their journey into the unknown, where the line between reality and gaming had become indistinguishable.

Eighteen

Of Love and Lumatores

The meeting had come to a close, plans solidified and preparations made for the coming journey. Helios and Aurora had stayed behind, still locked in a heated debate about her orders to remain in Lumora as acting captain. Lucy and Alex started walking toward the foyer, planning one last night out before their journey, when they were interrupted.

"Lucy, Alex, just a moment," Kaleigh's voice called from behind them. "My mother asked me to extend an invitation for dinner this evening, if you aren't busy."

"We were just talking about plans for the night," Lucy responded. "We were thinking about going to Sonata Square. I'm pretty sure I owe someone a dance. I sort of ruined the last one."

Kaleigh's eyes lit up. "That's perfect! My mother's home is only a block from the Square."

Alex looked at Lucy, who nodded wordlessly. "That settles it then. We'd be honored."

"Great! I'll show you..."

"YOU NEED ME OUT THERE!" Aurora's voice echoed from the meeting room.

"I need you here, Lieutenant!" Helios' voice was firm as he stressed every syllable of her rank, reminding her and everyone within hearing distance that he was the Captain of the Guard. "This city must not fall, and I trust nobody more than you to ensure its safety in my stead. Do you understand?"

Aurora looked as if she may protest again before begrudgingly backing down. "I understand, Captain. I don't like it, but I understand."

Helios, finally noticing the attention the argument had drawn, visibly calmed before speaking again. "Good. I hate pulling rank on you, Aurora. You're a damn fine officer and an even better friend, and I would love to have you at my back for this mission. But this city needs you more than I do. Keep the guard in line and our people safe, and we will end this."

Aurora nodded silently before rising from her seat. She took one last look at Helios, as if considering the merit of another objection, then turned and left the room.

As she approached, Kaleigh turned to her. "Rori, you know there's no better protector for this city than you." As she spoke, she brushed her fingers along Aurora's cheek. "With Helios gone, our people will need you."

Aurora turned, nuzzling her face into Kaleigh's hand. "I know Kaybee, I know. I just hate sending you all out there, not knowing what you'll find or face. If I lost you, any of you, and I could have prevented it…"

Kaleigh cupped Aurora's chin lightly, reaching up with her other hand to brush an errant lock of hair from her face. "If something happens out there, it won't be on you. You will be here, doing your job, and we will be out there doing ours." She kissed Aurora gently, speaking softly as she pulled away. "And nothing will happen to me. I have the Captain and the Lumatores to protect me."

Alex and Lucy watched in confusion as Kaleigh and Aurora laughed softly. "I feel like we missed something," Lucy said. "What's a Lumatore?"

Kaleigh turned back, smiling. "It's you. It means warrior of light."

Aurora grinned as she interjected. "She made it up."

Kaleigh lightly bumped Aurora with her hip, laughing. "It fits, though. Doesn't it? There has never been another who can do the things they can, so there's never been a word for it. Now there is."

Alex smiled at the banter between the two women. "Fair enough."

Lucy grinned at Kaleigh. "I kinda like it."

"Are they coming with us, Kay?" Aurora asked, taking Kaleigh's hand.

"They are." Kaleigh turned to Alex and Lucy. "Are you ready?"

Lucy smiled. "Lead the way."

***

As the group walked through the streets of Lumora, the music of Sonata Square began to break through the eerie silence. Much of the city was quiet these days, the fading of the Conflux and the Mother's light casting a shadow of dread over the people of Lumora. Many stayed inside, remained hidden in fear of the blight.

But the people of Sonata Square were not so easily broken. The Square was a place filled with spirit and expression, and its people would not be intimidated into giving up so easily. The artists and craftspeople of Sonata Square would continue to live fully, until there was nothing left.

Lucy started swaying to the gentle sounds, getting caught up in the harmonies and rhythms. "I could really get used to this every night."

"So could I." Alex took Lucy's hands in his, swaying along with her.

Their moment was quickly disturbed by a commotion behind them, as Aurora's voice overtook the music.

"I am nothing to you! You proved that years ago."

The man standing in front of Aurora said something in a low voice, attempting to grab her arm as he did. Aurora pulled her arm away from him violently. "Touch me again, and it may well be the last thing you ever do."

Kaleigh stepped forward at this, her eyes wild. She began to speak, but the man cut her off with a wave of his hand. "You stay out of this girl! This whole situation is your fault. You did this to her!"

Alex, fueled by his own share of father issues, walked quickly to Aurora's side. "Mr. Artisynth, I presume?"

The older man, nearly a foot taller than Alex, sneered at the interruption.

Alex held out his hand in greeting. "Alex Porter. Nice to meet you."

Aeros Artisynth levied his full gaze on Alex then. Disregarding the outstretched hand, he looked down at Alex as he would an insect. "It does not matter to me who you are. This does not concern you, outsider." It was a withering gaze that Alex was faced with, and he was certain that it had worked on many before him. But this was no ordinary night, and Alex was no ordinary outsider. Not anymore.

Alex smiled back at the man in front of him, the air of superiority almost amusing as it reminded him of his own father. "I'm afraid it does. You see..."

Aeros rolled his eyes as he attempted to sidestep Alex, but Alex stepped in front of him. "I am talking to you!" Alex's smile faltered as his anger rose.

"How dare you..." Aeros' words stopped abruptly as fear slackened his face, illuminated by a blue glow from the lightning flashing in Alex's eyes.

"I believe my friend, and her lovely girlfriend, have made it very clear. Stay." he took a step forward, causing Aeros to stumble back. "The fuck." Another step, another stumble. "Away!"

Aeros tripped over a loose stone, barely keeping his footing. He glared at Alex as he straightened himself, the effect lessened by the fear still evident. "This is not the end of this, outsider!"

"Lumatore," Alex said calmly. "The word you're looking for is Lumatore."

His eyes flared again for emphasis, and Aeros turned and nearly ran in fear. Alex watched the arrogant Mr. Artisynth until he was out of sight, then turned to find the stunned expressions of Aurora and Kaleigh.

"H-How did you…" Kaleigh began. "How did you do that?"

"Do what?"

"You just… you called the light…" Kaleigh stuttered. "And then you… you just swallowed it back into yourself. How did you do that?"

"Is that not normal? You can't do that?"

Kaleigh shook her head slowly. "Alex, nobody can do that. My mother can't even do that. When a Lumarch summons the light, it must be discharged in some way. If not, it can consume us. It can destroy us." She shook her head in disbelief. "Do you have any idea how much control it takes to do what you did? Because I don't. It's never been done before."

Kaleigh then wheeled on Lucy. "Can you do that too?"

"Kaleigh. My only lesson was today, remember? I have no idea what I can do yet."

"Right. Of course." Kaleigh shook her head as if trying to regain her senses. "I'm sorry. I'm freaking out a little. This is…" She looked back at Alex, the awe in her face joined by excitement. "This is incredible."

Lucy flashed Alex a grin, cocking an eyebrow. "It was pretty damn hot, if you ask me."

"Alex," Aurora said softly. "Why?"

Alex turned to look at her, seeing a mixture of sadness and anger in her face. She had been silent, withdrawn in the moments since her father's departure. In the moment, it never occurred to him that he was overstepping his bounds. He saw a friend being bullied by her father, just like he had been for so long, and he had to make it stop. "I'm sorry Aurora. I know you can handle yourself. I just…"

Alex's words were cut off as he was suddenly wrapped in a hug. "Thank you. Nobody has ever talked to him like that, especially for me." She pulled away, wiping at her eyes with her sleeve as a smile spread across her face. "And it's Rori, damn it. Don't make me remind you again."

Alex put his hands up in mock surrender. "Yes, ma'am." He let his hands drop as his face softened. "We all care about you, Rori. If he wants to come after you, he deals with all of us. Not to mention," the corners of his mouth curled slightly, "he's a dick. It was my pleasure."

Aurora let out a laugh, chasing away the last remnants of sadness and anger from her face. "So true, Alex. So very true."

***

Alex and Lucy sat next to each other at a round table in the center of a small, but elegant dining room. Aurora and Kaleigh sat opposite them, laughing together at one of their many inside jokes. An older woman sat nearest to the kitchen door, smiling contently as she watched her daughter. She was wrapped in violet robes, a symbol of her authority as a Lumarch elder. Her watchful, crystalline eyes were identical to Kaleigh's, save for the darkened blue bolts of the light's mark.

"Thank you so much for inviting us to dinner, Mrs. Britewaith. Do you need any help cleaning up?" Alex offered with a smile.

"First, please call me Valia, dear. And you stay right where you are. My home will take care of it." As if on cue, the dinnerware on the table began glowing before levitating above their heads and leaving the room.

"Your home is alive too?" Lucy asked.

"No, not exactly. Not to the extent of the palace. I've simply added a few enchantments here and there to help around the house."

"She learned that trick as soon as I was old enough to walk. Go figure." Kaleigh interjected, grinning mischievously. "My father is a neat freak. Speaking of, I thought Dad was supposed to be here for dinner?"

"You know your father. Always caught up in one project or another. I made him promise to be here to see you off, before you go..." Valia trailed off, her eyes haunted by the possibilities. She quickly recovered as she continued. "Anyway, you know that man hasn't broken a promise in the forty years I've known him. He'll be here."

"He's nothing, if not reliable."

Alex felt a pang of envy at Kaleigh's words. A glance at Aurora, their eyes meeting in shared understanding, proved to Alex that he wasn't alone.

"What is he working on tonight?" Kaleigh had missed the pained glances shared across the table. Lucy had not.

Lucy placed a hand on Alex's arm, worry shading her face as she looked at him. Leaning in, she whispered to him softly. "What's wrong?"

Alex shook his head, forcing a smile. "Just a moment of understanding between friends," he whispered back. "I'll tell you all about it later, if you want to know."

Lucy nodded and kissed his cheek. "I want to know everything."

"Is something wrong?" Valia asked, noticing the tension and hushed tones beside her.

"No, not at all Valia," Alex responded. "All this talk of Mr. Britewaith just reminded me of a rather unpleasant encounter we had on our way here."

"My father, unfortunately," Aurora added.

"Oh, that miserable grayscale… he was never a father to you!" Her fury softened as she looked at Aurora. "I'm sorry, dear, but that man had no business raising a child. I should have taken you in the day your mother passed."

"To be fair," Kaleigh interrupted, "I'm certain that today's experience was far more troubling for him than it was for us, thanks to Alex."

Valia smiled as her attention shifted back to Alex. "Ah, a true hero already, are we?"

Alex laughed. "Hardly. I just don't like bullies."

"Hardly?" Kaleigh all but shrieked. "Are you forgetting what happened out there?" She turned excitedly to Valia, nearly jumping from her chair. "Mom, you will never believe this. I watched Alex quell the light."

The Lumarch elder looked as if she had taken a blow, an odd sight given that she seemed to be a woman who wasn't surprised often. "That's not possible."

"That's what I thought too, but he did it. He called the light, it flashed in his eyes, scared the shit out of old Aeros, then Alex just… just absorbed it back in."

"Well then. You certainly are full of surprises, Alex. As a Lumarch elder, I really should warn you of such use of your power. The Mother gives us our light to help people, and using the light in such a manner is reckless and dangerous.

That being said, I am both impressed with your control, and disappointed that I didn't get to watch Aeros squirm."

Lucy smirked at the older woman. "You wouldn't happen to be friends with Queen Celestia, would you?"

"As a matter of fact, we've always been quite close, ever since we were children. How did you know?"

Lucy shrugged. "Lucky guess."

The room settled into a comfortable rhythm of conversation as they shared stories and anecdotes, with Valia occasionally interjecting her wisdom. Kaleigh and Aurora's love for each other was palpable, their gentle touches and shared smiles speaking of the depth of their connection. It was a bond that had spanned many years apart and still held true. It was inspiring to watch.

As the evening drew to a close, Valia turned her gaze toward Alex. "I hope you've enjoyed the meal and the company, dear. You have a long journey ahead of you. Remember that you and Lucy have been a source of light and hope for our world. You both carry a tremendous burden, but also great potential."

Alex nodded, grateful for her words of encouragement. "We'll do our best to live up to the faith you put in us, Valia."

Alex and Lucy left Valia's home with hearts full of gratitude and a deepening sense of purpose. They walked hand in hand through the streets of Lumora, guided by the soft glow of the city's lights. Sonata Square was alive with music, laughter, and dancing, and the couple couldn't resist its allure. Lucy turned to Alex with a mischievous glint in her eyes. "I think it's time we make up for that dance I owe you."

Alex grinned and pulled her closer. "Good, I've been waiting for this."

Their movements were harmonious, the worries of the world temporarily forgotten as their bodies swayed to the music. As they danced under the starry sky of Lumora, the world around them shimmered with magic and possibilities. The blight and the blurring line between reality and the virtual realm no longer seemed daunting; it was an adventure they were ready to face together.

Nineteen

Armor and Affection

Alex woke to golden light streaming through the stained glass of the balcony door, the sun barely breaking over the horizon. Lucy still slept at his side, her face serene and peaceful, the weight of the day unable to reach her in her dreams. Alex gently moved closer to lay a kiss on her forehead, taking in the floral scent of her hair.

Leaving Lucy to her precious few remaining moments of peace, Alex carefully swung his legs over the side of the bed and stood. He took in the chill of the stone floor beneath his feet, many of the palace's comforts having been foregone simply for the sake of the Conflux's survival. It was yet another bitter reminder of the coming days, of what they would be fighting for.

Alex quietly padded across the stone slabs of the chamber into the washroom. Stripping off his bedclothes, he stepped into the large shower stall, allowing the lukewarm water to rain down over his body. Alex reflected on the last week of

162

his suddenly hectic life, the whirlwind of emotions and adventures he had experienced in such a short time. He thought about his new friends, closer to him than anyone ever cared to get before. He thought about the love that he had never thought he would find. Above all, Alex thought about how he could lose everything he had gained in the coming days.

Deep in thought, Alex jumped when he felt a pair of delicate hands slide around his ribs, resting on his chest.

"Are you okay?" Lucy asked cautiously from behind him.

"You just surprised me. I was… distracted."

"Of course. Well, I was thinking," Lucy said in his ear, placing a light kiss on his neck just behind his right ear, "that maybe we should conserve water. You know, for the good of the Conflux."

Alex let out a soft moan as the heat of her breath caressed his neck. She pressed the length of her body against his back, slick with the water falling over them, as her right hand trailed down his stomach. Electricity flowed from her touch, a ripple moving from her lips on his neck down to lower places.

"Right," he said, his voice forced from his quickened breath, "for the Conflux."

Alex turned in Lucy's arms, pressing himself against her as he buried his face into her neck. His hands slid down the length of her back until his fingertips brushed the sensitive skin just below. His lips moved with precision as he kissed from her collarbone to her earlobe, and every inch in between.

"Alex." His name came out as a moan. "Alex," she said again in a raspy tone, but this time strong enough to get his attention. She pulled away slightly, just enough to look into his eyes. "I am in love with you. With everything going on, I need you to know that. If this is going to be our last moment alone before… I need this, Alex. I need you… all of you."

"You have all of me, Lucy. Heart, soul…" He looked down with a grin. "Body. Name it, and it's yours."

Lucy's face shifted slightly, and the look she gave Alex told him exactly what she wanted in that moment. "Why don't I show you instead?"

***

Helios, Aurora, and Kaleigh were already waiting in the armory when Alex and Lucy arrived, determined faces turning toward them as they entered. The room was dimly lit, the air heavy with tension as the group prepared for their journey.

Alex and Lucy exchanged a weighty glance, their shared conviction etched across their faces. They knew the gravity of their mission, the uncertainty that lay ahead, and the strength of the bond that united them. It would be enough. It had to be enough.

Silently, Alex helped Lucy into the light plate armor she had chosen, thanking the Mother that she had opted for extra protection over mobility. He fiddled with the straps and buckles until the armor was fully secured, then moved on to his own leather armor.

Aurora stepped forward to assist, her uniform exuding an air of authority. Her gaze locked onto Alex and Lucy, her voice firm but filled with worry. "Remember, the stakes are higher than we've ever faced. This journey won't be without its dangers, but Lumora depends on your success."

Alex nodded, his voice steady. "We understand, Aurora. We will end this, for both worlds, and for those here we have come to love."

Lucy nodded. "We won't let you down."

Kaleigh approached with a small, ornate box in her hands, its lid intricately designed with the Lumoran crest. She opened it, revealing two luminescent crystals affixed to silver chains. The smooth, milky surface of the crystals emitted a soft, calming light. "These are Lumorethian Crystals, passed down through generations of Lumarchs before us. Mine," she paused with a hand on her heart, fingers tracing the smooth edges of her crystal, "came to me when my grandmother passed away. They serve as a focus for the light, something of a rechargeable battery, you might say. They are also a symbol of our unity with each other, and with the Mother. Wear them close to your heart, so you never forget her love. May their light shine in the darkest of times."

Alex and Lucy accepted the crystals, their hands trembling slightly as they felt the warmth emanating from within. The significance of the moment was clear to them, even though the custom was not.

Helios, always the embodiment of stoic strength, finally broke his silence. "Remember, you are not alone. The entire city stands with you, and we will be by your side. Trust in your abilities, and in each other."

Aurora placed one hand on Alex's shoulder, the other on Lucy's, a silent assurance of her support. "I watched you enter our world with a courage you didn't believe you had. Yet, even since then, you have both become formidable in so many ways. You have our trust and our hearts. Bring back the light, my friends," Aurora said, her voice filled with both pride and anxiety. "And please bring Kay back to me. I can't lose her again."

Lucy pulled her into a hug. "We'll do everything in our power to bring everyone home, Rori. I wish I could promise more, but it's all I have."

Alex watched a tear roll down Aurora's cheek, and in that moment, he realized everything she was sacrificing. Sending away the love she only recently reconnected with, along with her captain and friend? Putting their fate in the hands of two outsiders who were mere strangers a week ago? The weight of it staggered him, his own eyes misting slightly.

As Lucy pulled away from Aurora, Alex moved in to hug her as well, whispering to her as he did, "she will come back to you. I'll give everything in me to make it happen."

Aurora pulled back from the hug, a small smile on her face. "I know you will, Alex. And you had better be with her, all of you, or I'll hunt you down in the afterlife and kick your asses."

Aurora turned to stand at attention in front of Helios. "Captain."

"Lieutenant." Helois responded stiffly. His face softened as he looked at his second in command, his friend. He smiled as he continued. "Rori, the Captain bars suit you. I could have known no better second. Keep our city safe in my absence."

"I will, Helios. I will try to serve with the bravery and honor that the station demands. That you have brought to it."

Helios wrapped her in a tight hug, clapping her on the back as he said, "You already do, my friend."

Pulling away, Helios pounded a fist to his chest, the

clanging of his armor echoing through the armory, and bowed to Aurora before joining Alex and Lucy in their final preparations.

Alex stood beside Lucy, looking on as Aurora led Kaleigh to the corner of the room to share a private farewell. Moments later they watched as Aurora kissed Kaleigh one last time and left, Kaleigh watching helplessly as she walked away.

Alex felt Lucy's hand slide into his. "I don't know if we'll be ready for what we find, Alex," Lucy's voice echoed his own thoughts, "but at least we get to face it together."

"Oh, thank the Mother. I saw the Lieutenant in the hall and worried you might have already left." Queen Celestia's voice rang out from the doorway. She approached Helios, arms outstretched. She placed her hands on the pauldrons of his armor, pulling her into him. "Lios, I have never been so proud to have you not listen to me. I understand now why you must go. Your father and Aureon would be proud as well."

Helios wrapped his arms around Celestia. "Thank you, Mother. It means a great deal to me that you feel that way."

"I love you, Lios. You've always had such a big heart, and courage to match. I know you will end this blight and bring everyone home safely."

"And you, Kaleigh," Celestia turned to the Lumarch. "Thank you for joining this cause. Your wisdom and knowledge have been invaluable to this city. May your light shine brightly, Lumarch Britewaith."

Kaleigh bowed deeply. "It has been an honor, your Majesty."

Finally, Celestia stood before Alex and Lucy. "And you, our Lumadores, if I am informed correctly?"

Lucy grinned at Kaleigh. "Well, I guess that's stuck."

The Queen laughed. "I hope you like it, because my understanding is that it has been spread throughout the city. Shall we simply call you what you are? Our heroes. You were thrust into this world with no warning or connections, yet you chose to fight for us. You have shown the compassion, love, and inspiration of true Lumorans, and true Lumorans you now are. This is your home now, too, if you wish it. To that point, I took the liberty of commissioning something for both of you."

Celestia produced two small wooden boxes from her pockets and handed one to each of them. Alex opened the box to find a beautifully crafted silver ring adorned with the majestic lion of Lumora's crest. Behind the lion, a beautifully etched representation of the Prisma Staff lined in tiny glowing crystals. Lucy's ring was nearly identical, save for the crossed blades, her Starfall Sabers, replacing the staff.

Alex placed the ring on his hand, the crystals flaring as he touched the smooth metal. Then, placing his fist to his chest, he took a knee before Celestia. "Thank you, my queen. I will do everything I can for our city."

Lucy followed his lead soon after. "We are honored, my queen, by your generosity and honor."

Celestia stood in silence for a moment. "I truly appreciate the sentiment, but would you two please get up and give me a hug?"

Alex and Lucy stood, wrapping the Queen in their arms. "You two are family now. Please be safe and watch out for each other. Keep an eye on Lios, and take care of Kaleigh. If anything happens to her, I will have her mother and my acting captain to answer to. I do not think I need to tell you how poorly that conversation would go." Celestia kissed Lucy's forehead, then Alex's. "I love you both. Good luck."

Celestia strode for the door to the armory, stopping at the threshold for one final glance back at the group. She lingered a moment longer, then turned and left.

A quiet fell amongst the group, a contemplative silence. For Alex, it was a silence born of the understanding that goodbyes were finished, preparations made, and all that was left to do was to begin the journey. He had pushed the nerves aside from the second he woke, but they took hold in this moment. A wave of fear and doubt that he had been trying so hard to hold at bay suddenly flooded through him. But it was too late to turn back now. Time was up, and they were out of options.

Helios finally broke the silence. "Are we ready to depart?"

Alex laughed nervously. "No, but let's do it, anyway."

Nerves finally caught up to you, too? Lucy's voice echoed in Alex's mind.

Alex looked at her and nodded wordlessly, before saying aloud, "We're as ready as we can be for something like this. Let's move."

Twenty

Harmony in Chaos

Helios led the small band as they emerged from the armored doors of the palace, their footsteps echoing through the grand corridor. The city of Lumora, with its glowing spires and bustling streets, lay stretched out before them. The sun had fully risen, casting a radiant glow over the magnificent city that had become their home in a remarkably short time.

For Alex and Lucy, the sight of Lumora's beauty contrasted starkly with the burden of their impending journey. They felt a profound sense of attachment to this world and its people, an unspoken promise to protect what had been so graciously offered.

As they walked through the streets, the people of Lumora lined their path, offering words of encouragement, gratitude, and hope. The entire city stood behind them, their unwavering support a testament to the bond that had formed between the newcomers and the Lumorans.

Helios, resplendent in his polished armor, walked with an air of authority, acknowledging the well-wishers with a nod and a smile. Kaleigh, adorned in her Lumarch robes, radiated wisdom and grace, a symbol of Lumora's guidance and strength.

Alex and Lucy held hands, their eyes filled with a mix of anticipation and apprehension. They smiled back at the cheering crowds, feeling the warmth of the Lumorans' love and solidarity. The atmosphere was one of unity, a collective determination to restore light to the city and reclaim what had been lost.

Helios hesitated for a moment as they turned the corner leading to the city gates. Alex followed his gaze to find the road ahead lined with what seemed to be the entire guard corps. Each uniformed Lumoran held a gloved fist to their chest, a sign of respect and honor that brought with it a flood of emotion over the four companions.

As the group approached, a single guard broke from the ranks, standing before Helios with his head bowed. A familiar voice spoke in his most official tone. "Cap'n, with yer permission, I'd like ta' speak direc'ly with tha' Lumadores."

Helios nodded. "Permission granted." Helios stepped to the side, and Auril stepped forward, dropping to a knee. "Lumadores, I owe ya' both an apology. There's no excuse fer my rudeness when ya' first arrived. What yer doin' here, fer us…"

Alex offered a hand and pulled Auril to his feet. "No apology needed, Auril. Your support, here and now, is what matters most to me."

Auril nodded, then returned to his place in the formation.

Helios cocked an eyebrow at Alex. "Do you know how hard it is to get an apology out of him?" he asked quietly. "You truly are full of surprises."

The group continued their march to the gates, Alex smiling at Auril as they passed. The military-like parade through the street was a surreal experience for Alex. But then again, that made it no different from the events of the entire week before.

Aurora stood at attention atop the wall, watching over the parapet as the four travelers approached. Helios stopped short of the gates, looking up at her. He spoke in a thundering voice, the unmistakable authority echoing through the streets. "You all know what is at stake for us. The Lumigenesis Conflux is fading. The Mother is weak. But she has given us two champions willing to fight for us." He paused as cheers erupted from the guards, causing an immediate blush to form on the cheeks of both Alex and Lucy. "You remain here to protect this city. There is no telling what threats we face, both at our gates and abroad. But we will face these threats, we will prevail, and we will restore our way of life."

Helios then stood at attention, fist to his chest, as he addressed Aurora directly. "Captain?"

Immediately, Aurora's voice boomed out, matching the authority of Helios' words. "Open the gates!" A barely perceptible hint of sadness showed in her eyes as she looked down at them. Her lips moved again, soundlessly this time, mouthing the words *"be safe"*. Kaleigh put two fingers to her lips and raised them toward Aurora, then followed as the group moved ahead to the path beyond.

***

"It's hard to believe this all started a week ago, in those woods." Lucy flashed a grin at Alex before continuing. "Maybe the trees just needed a hug. Go ahead, Alex. You're the expert."

Alex gave her a sardonic smile as he thought back to their first encounter. It felt like so long ago after everything they had been through. "Remind me, who was it that figured out how to unlock that tree's power?"

It was early afternoon when the group first stopped for rest and food. They stood at the base of the ridge where the Whispering Wood had nearly taken Alex, where they had first met Helios and Aurora. The nearest trees were still scorched from the fire arrows raining down on them.

Alex looked at Helios. "What happened to the new guy? The archer? I haven't seen him since that day."

Helios smiled. "Phelan? Turns out he was too good an archer to waste on simple guard duty. I had him promoted to instructor. He's been spending all his time working with recruits."

Alex smiled back. "Good to hear. He was quiet, but he seemed like a decent guy. Whiskers liked him, which is usually a good sign."

"He's a good kid. He's had some tough times, but it hasn't slowed him down any. Lost his parents when he was a child. Grew up with his grandmother. He got married at a young age, then lost his new wife in childbirth."

"That's awful," Lucy said.

"It is. If I'm being honest, it's one of the reasons I promoted him. Not pity, mind you, but because he now takes care of his elderly grandmother and an infant by himself, and still he is one of the most selfless and compassionate people I've ever met. He deserved the recognition, and he needed the money."

"It's nice to see that some places still value such traits," Alex said wistfully.

Helios nodded in agreement. "In Lumora, character and compassion have always been highly regarded qualities. It's not just about strength and power, but the goodness of one's heart."

Kaleigh chimed in, "The ability to care for others and put their needs before your own is what makes a true Lumoran."

As they continued their journey, the landscape shifted from the familiarity of the Whispering Wood to the wild, uncharted territories that lay beyond Lumora's borders. They followed a rugged path, winding and nearly overgrown. Helios led the way, his senses alert to any potential threats.

Lucy, walking alongside Kaleigh, couldn't help but marvel at the natural beauty that surrounded them. "It's incredible how the world can change so quickly. One moment we're in a city of light, and the next, we're in the heart of nature."

Kaleigh's eyes sparkled as she gazed at the untouched wilderness. "Lumora is a unique place, connected to both nature and the cosmos. The harmony between our world and the Mother's gift creates something truly special."

As they walked further into the untamed wilderness, the air filled with the fragrances of wildflowers. The sounds of chirping of birds and the distant rushing of a river echoed around them. The magnificence of nature filled their senses, reminding them of the delicate balance that existed in the world.

Lucy felt a sense of serenity and connection as she took in the surrounding beauty. "You know, I've always been a bit of a city girl. I've never really spent much time in nature like this, but I'm beginning to see the appeal. It's breathtaking."

Kaleigh nodded. "It's a reminder of the simple, profound beauty of our world. We're in a place where the Mother's touch is everywhere, and it's a powerful symbol of what we're fighting for."

Suddenly, a low growl emanated from the underbrush. All eyes snapped in the direction of the sound as an enormous, graceful creature emerged. Its body nearly dragged on the ground, its thick, muscular legs splayed to its sides. The thick, leathery skin of the twelve foot reptilian creature was a sickly green with blackened tendrils along its back. A whip-like tail flicked about as the mouth of it's diamond-shaped head snapped in anger.

Alex immediately stepped back. "What is that thing?"

Kaleigh responded, her voice shaking slightly. "It... It looks like a Lumoray, but..."

"Wait, I read about those. They're supposed to be docile, right?"

"They're supposed to be," Kaleigh responded unconvincingly.

The Lumoray lunged at the group, its movements swift and aggressive, and the four quickly drew their weapons, ready to defend themselves.

The Lumoray's first target was Lucy, who was slightly separated from the others. With a ferocious snap of its razor sharp teeth, it clamped onto her leg, causing her to cry out in pain. The creature's fangs pierced her flesh, but her light armor offered some protection. It was a painful injury, but not life-threatening.

Alex reacted swiftly, his staff coming down to deliver a blow to the back of the Lumoray, causing it to release Lucy and roar in agony. Kaleigh and Helios joined the fight, their attacks weakening the creature.

Lucy attempted to stand, determined to join the fight, but the tearing sensation of the wound made it nearly unbearable. Still, she managed to get to her feet and, seeing that the creature had focused now on Alex, she took the opportunity to strike from behind.

She crouched in an attack stance, all of her weight placed on her uninjured leg. As her swords crossed in front of her, Lucy's eyes flared with blue lightning. She drew one blade along the length of the other in a long, deliberate stroke. Blue flame engulfed the scimitar as she pounced forward, raising the weapon above her head and driving it through the spine of the Lumoray, straight into its heart.

The creature bucked wildly with the blow, Lucy holding the sword handle firmly to avoid being thrown. Its tail thrashed overhead in an attempt to knock Lucy away, but the beast was weakening rapidly. Soon, the bucking stopped altogether as the creature's blood soaked the patchy grass and dirt below, leaving it limp on the damp ground.

Lucy rolled off the Lumoray's back, thudding on the ground with a groan, and Kaleigh was immediately kneeling beside her.

"It looks bad, but I don't think it's very deep," Kaleigh said. The palms of her hands glowed a pale blue as she held them over the wound. "No, not deep at all. This should…" Kaleigh stopped, turning slowly to stare at Lucy incredulously.

"What?" Alex almost yelled. "What's wrong Kaleigh?"

Kaleigh gathered herself and looked back to Alex. "No, nothing wrong. I think I sense a piece of tooth or something in the wound. Could you and Helios please check the packs for my forceps?"

Alex rushed to find the dropped packs with Helios in tow. Kaleigh organized her pack well, so Alex was able to find the tool quickly and return it to the healer.

Lucy's face had paled since he left only moments ago. He passed the forceps to Kaleigh absentmindedly as he kneeled at Lucy's side. "Are you okay? Is it the blood loss?" He turned to Kaleigh. "Lumorays aren't venomous, are they?"

Lucy put a hand on Alex's shoulder. "Alex, I'm fine. Kaleigh will take care of me, and I'll be fine."

"I'm sorry, Lucy," Kaleigh interrupted, "but this might hurt a little."

Alex offered his hand, which Lucy accepted gratefully. She stifled a scream and squeezed Alex's hand as Kaleigh slid the forceps deep into the wound, extracting a small shard of a pointed tooth.

"Sorry, sorry. Hard part is over." Kaleigh's hands glowed once again, and skin and tissue began to knit back together. Moments later, only a light scar remained.

Lucy looked at Kaleigh with a strange mixture of fear and happiness that Alex didn't quite understand. "Thank you Kaleigh." She took Kaleigh's hand in hers, the two sharing an unspoken moment that confused Alex further. "For everything," Lucy finished.

After Kaleigh left to clean up, Alex looked at Lucy. The color was returning to her face, and she seemed more herself. Relieved, he said, "That was some move. And you said I was the badass."

"I never said I wasn't," Lucy replied, grinning. "You were pretty good, yourself. Chances are, I wouldn't have a leg if you hadn't moved so quickly. Kaleigh's good, but I don't think limb reattachments are quite as easy."

Alex bent down, kissing Lucy gently before helping her to her feet. "Does it hurt?"

Lucy tested her weight on the leg. "A little sore, but mostly fine. It shouldn't take long to finish healing."

"Good." Alex smiled at her. "We're lucky to have Kaleigh with us."

Lucy glanced at the Lumarch rinsing her hands in a nearby stream. "We are. We're very lucky she's here."

Twenty-One

Strength in Tears

Alex sat on a fallen log, warming by the fire. They had stopped to make camp shortly after the Lumoray attack, finding a clearing near the stream that allowed them plenty of room and visibility. Alex had volunteered to take first watch, opting to ensure that everyone, especially Lucy, had a chance to rest after the unexpected excitement. It also gave him a chance to be alone with his thoughts.

Alex had been worried about Lucy since the attack. The injury seemed relatively minor, and Kaleigh had healed it easily. Still, there was something the two seemed to be keeping from him. It hadn't occurred to him at the time, but Kaleigh always carried an emergency set of instruments on her. So there had to have been a reason for her to send him away.

Was the wound worse than they let on? Lucy seemed to be fine after. She had said it was just a bit sore, and she didn't seem to be favoring that leg when they set up camp. The Lumoray was typically extremely docile, almost friendly, unless provoked. Based on his reading, they weren't supposed to be venomous, but this one also had odd coloring compared to the details in the book. Maybe it was corrupted. Maybe it passed the corruption to Lucy. Is that what they didn't want to tell him?

He had so many questions, and each new thought was worse than the last. "Okay, I need to stop spiraling. Maybe it has nothing to do with Lucy's health at all. Maybe they just wanted to talk in private. They're entitled to privacy, right? If I needed to know, they'd tell me. I'm sure..."

Alex whirled around as he heard a voice behind him. "Alex, are you talking to yourself?" Helios was leaning on a tree, an amused smile on his face.

"No, I just... Yeah, I guess I am."

"Would you..." Helios stifled a laugh, "would you like me to leave so you can continue your, um, conversation?"

Alex rolled his eyes. "Funny, thanks. What are you doing up?"

Helios pointed up. "The moon is at its apex. It's time for shift change."

Alex stared at the moon as if it had just appeared. Had it been that long already? "Oh, okay. Right, then I guess... I guess I'll go get some rest."

As Alex turned to walk away, Helios' voice drew his attention back. "She's fine, you know. She has the Mother's protection, and Kaleigh is an excellent healer. Whatever they're keeping to themselves, I'm sure it's nothing to worry about."

Alex nodded, "You're right. Of course you're right. I just worry."

"Because you love her. I'd be concerned if you didn't."

Alex nodded again, then turned and walked to his bedroll, laying down next to Lucy and drifting off to sleep.

***

The first rays of daylight streamed across Alex's face as he woke. Blinking the sleep from his eyes, he turned away from the brightness to find an empty bedroll at his side. "Lucy?"

"Over here," Lucy said, standing by the dwindling fire. "I couldn't sleep, so I took the last watch. Turned out to be more eventful than I anticipated."

Alex sat up, following her gaze to the fallen log nearby. "Why? What's going..."

His thoughts were cut short when he saw a young girl sitting on the log in front of Lucy, wrapped in a blanket. Her dark blue skin was weathered from the elements, small cuts and bruises scattered across her face and hands. Her thick, dark hair was cut to shoulder length, tangled with twigs and leaves from her time in the woods.

Lucy looked at Alex, sadness filling her eyes. Using their telepathic link, she said, *I found her hiding in the brush. Poor girl is from a nearby farming village that got overtaken by the blight. She's the only one who made it out.*

Alex nodded solemnly, standing from his bedroll and walking slowly toward the girl. He crouched down in front of her, just out of reach. "Hi there. I'm Alex. What's your name?"

The girl burrowed further into the blanket, a pair of deep brown eyes staring intently as if peering into his soul.

"You don't have to tell me if you don't want to. But you're safe with us, I promise. We're here to help."

The girl stayed silent, still watching for any sign of ill

intent. Alex stood, turning to Lucy, when a small, muffled voice came from behind him.

"Are you.. Are you the Lumatores?"

Alex turned back, smiling, and crouched down again. "You've heard of us? Way out here?"

A small face poked out of the blanket, the beginnings of a toothy grin now visible. "Everyone's heard about the Lumatores. My momma told me all about how you're gonna save the world."

"We're sure going to try, sweetie," Lucy said, crouching next to Alex.

"Ilya. My name's Ilya."

"Nice to meet you, Ilya." Alex offered his hand, and her small hand emerged tentatively to take it. "Like I said, I'm Alex, and you already met Lucy. She's really nice, right?"

Ilya nodded enthusiastically. "And pretty, just like my momma."

Alex's smile widened. "She is really pretty, isn't she? She's also really strong. I guarantee she won't let anything bad happen to you. Neither will I, or our friends."

Ilya's jaw dropped in astonishment. In a near whisper, she asked, "Is she stronger than you?"

Alex nodded. "She's stronger than anyone. She got bit by a monster yesterday, and even hurt, she still saved us all."

"Wow..." Ilya looked at Lucy, eyes wide. "That's so cool. You're a hero."

"Well," Lucy said, "Alex is exaggerating a little bit. He saved me first."

Ilya looked between Lucy and Alex curiously. "Are you two in love?"

Alex was taken aback by the question. With a chuckle, he asked, "Why would you ask that?"

"'Cause you act like my momma and daddy do when they're together." She giggled as she continued. "They get all weird and say nice things about each other, too."

Alex and Lucy shared a grin, then Lucy said, "He is really weird, huh?" Ilya giggled again. "But yes, we are in love."

"Maybe that's why you're both so strong. My momma always says that love is stronger than anything in the world."

"I think you might be right," Lucy said, smiling. "Your momma sounds like a very smart woman."

Ilya's bright face suddenly darted back into the blanket as Helios' voice filled the clearing. "What's going on here?"

Alex put up a hand as Helios approached cautiously, hand on the hilt of his sword. He waved Helios further from the girl and followed. "She's just a little girl," he began once they were out of earshot. "Her entire village was wiped out by the blight. She's the only one who got out."

Helios looked stricken, a mix of sadness and anger in his eyes. "The entire... Her parents?"

Alex lowered his eyes, shaking his head sharply. He couldn't bring himself to say it out loud.

Helios turned his attention to Ilya, fury seething in his face as his hand tightened on his sword hilt. He looked back at Alex, shaking his head. "We need to end this now! That little girl has nobody left because of this corruption, and we don't even know yet what's causing it. We need to figure this out!"

Alex put a hand on Helios' shoulder. "And we will. I promise you, we will figure it out, but right now, we have a terrified little girl with no family left, and we need to stay calm so we can keep her calm."

"Of course. I'm sorry, you're absolutely right." Helios visibly relaxed as he looked back at the girl. "What's her name? I'd like to speak with her."

"Her name is Ilya. We haven't gotten a last name yet. Come on, I'll introduce you."

Alex led Helios back to the log where Ilya was sitting and eased down next to her. "Ilya, my friend would like to apologize for scaring you. Would you like to talk to him?"

A small voice came from the folds of the blanket. "Will you and Miss Lucy stay with me?"

Lucy sat on the other side of Ilya, putting an arm around her. "Of course we will, sweetie."

A moment passed quietly before Ilya reemerged from the blanket. "Okay, I can talk to him."

Helios stepped forward and took a knee in front of the child. "Hello, Ilya. Do you know who I am?"

Ilya nodded. "You're the Prince, right?"

Helios smiled wistfully. "Technically true, but I am also Captain of the Guard. You can call me Helios, though."

"I heard Momma tell Daddy once that she would leave him for you if you asked her to. I'm not sure what that meant, but they both laughed, so I think it was a grownup joke."

Helios let out a roar of laughter that instantly pulled a wide grin from Ilya's face. "I'm sure it was, little one. Your mother sounds a lot like mine."

"My momma is a queen?" Ilya looked shocked.

Helios laughed again. "No Ilya, what I mean is that she

sounds like a strong, wise, funny, and loving woman, just like the Queen is."

"Ilya, sweetheart." Lucy interrupted. "Are you okay here with Alex and Helios? I just want to get our other friend. She has magic that can fix those scrapes and bruises for you."

Ilya nodded. "I'm okay Miss Lucy."

Lucy left the little girl with Alex and Helios to wake Kaleigh and give her a brief report of the morning's events. Moments later, the two women came back to the group.

"Hi Ilya. I'm Kaleigh. Do you want to see some magic?"

Ilya had huddled partially back into the blanket at the sight of another new face, but the idea of magic was far too enticing for a child to ignore. She nodded emphatically as she looked up at Kaleigh.

"May I see your hand?" Kaleigh asked, holding her own hand out to the girl.

Tentatively, a small hand pushed through the layers of blanket and rested in Kaleigh's palm. Kaleigh put her free hand on top, palm glowing blue. When Kaleigh took her hand back, the scratches and bruises were gone.

Ilya stared at her now healed hand in awe. "That was amazing," she said, in a near whisper, as she slowly looked up at Kaliegh. "I wish I had magic."

"Who says you don't?" Kaleigh replied. "Sometimes magic takes some time to develop. I didn't get my magic until I was older than you."

"You mean, I might get magic when I'm older?"

"It's possible. The Mother gives to those who wish to serve others. Are you one of those people?"

Ilya grinned. "I like to help people. My momma says I'm

really helpful in the kitchen. And I help my daddy on the farm when the berries are ready to pick. I eat a few, too, but my daddy says he used to do the same thing when he was little. He says there's plenty to sell, so there's no harm in eating a few. Oh, and last week Mrs. Scatterbright's woolies got loose, and I helped her get them back in their pen."

Kaleigh smiled at the excited young girl. "It certainly sounds like you have the makings of a Lumarch. Perhaps the Mother will one day agree. But for now, I think we should get you some food. What do you think?"

Ilya nodded, her hands going to her stomach. "Yes, please. I'm really hungry."

Kaleigh reached into her pack and retrieved a wrapped piece of bread. She handed it to Ilya, who accepted it with a look of sheer delight.

"Thank you, Miss Kaleigh. This bread smells delicious," Ilya said before taking a hearty bite.

Alex, Helios, and Lucy exchanged smiles as they watched Ilya eat. Despite the dire circumstances, there was something heartwarming about this moment, a reminder of the goodness that could still be found even in the darkest of times.

After Ilya finished her bread, Kaleigh offered her a waterskin to quench her thirst. As the girl drank, Kaleigh finished healing her wounds. Finishing the water she had been offered, Ilya looked around at her new companions with curiosity.

"Where are we going?" Ilya asked.

Helios kneeled beside her. "We're on a journey to try to make the world a better place, to save everyone from the blight. We'll probably end up having to fight some monsters along the way. You're a brave girl who's been through a lot already, and I wish there was a better way, but for now, you'll have to come with us."

Ilya's eyes widened with surprise. "I am?"

Lucy nodded. "Yes, sweetie, you are. We'll make sure you're safe and taken care of."

Tears welled up in Ilya's eyes, and she threw her arms around Lucy. "Thank you so much. I'll help any way I can."

Lucy hugged the girl tightly. "No, Ilya. You're very brave, and very strong, but I need you to listen to me. We don't know what we're going to find, and so many people have already been hurt. If we tell you to run, you run. If we tell you to hide, you hide. We will keep you safe, but you need to do what we say. Do you understand?"

Ilya looked up at Lucy. "You really are like my momma, huh? She told me to run and hide in the woods when the darkness came. She made me go so I would be safe. She stayed with Daddy to fight, so I would be safe." Tears fell in streams down Ilya's face as she spoke. She buried her face in Lucy's side as she sobbed, "I'm never going to see them again, am I?"

Lucy stroked Ilya's hair softly. "I... I don't know, sweetheart. I'm so sorry, but I don't know."

Alex wrapped his arms around them both, his heart breaking for the girl who had seemed so hopeful only moments ago. Together, Alex and Lucy held Ilya, soothing her softly as she cried.

Ilya calmed after a while, running her blanketed arm across her face to wipe away the tears. "I'm sorry for being sad. I'm trying to be strong, but it's hard."

Alex looked down at the girl in his arms. "Never apologize for having emotions, Ilya. Real strength isn't about hiding your feelings. I cry sometimes. So does Lucy. Do you think that makes us less strong?"

Ilya looked up at Alex, then Lucy. "You do? My momma used to cry sometimes when we didn't have much money, and my daddy would tell her to be strong. I always thought that meant you weren't supposed to cry."

"No, Ilya," Lucy said. "Your daddy was just trying to make your momma feel better. There's nothing wrong with feeling sad sometimes. I know your momma was strong, because she raised a strong little girl who ran into the woods by herself and found help."

A pensive look crossed Ilya's face, then she nodded. "I think you're right. Momma fought for me, and she worked hard on our farm. I think she was really strong." Ilya looked around the campsite, taking in the faces of everyone around her. "So, when are we going?"

"As soon as you're ready, little one," Helios replied.

"Okay, let's go then."

The group broke camp quickly, more motivated than ever to find the source of the corruption that had taken so much from so many people. An entire village, wiped out. A little girl, likely orphaned and left to survive the woods on her own. The corruption of this land had gone on for far too long, and it needed to be stopped.

Soon, they were moving once again, keen eyes scanning their surroundings for any dangers. Ilya held Lucy's hand as they walked along the path. The group felt a renewed sense of purpose with their new charge at their sides, Ilya's presence serving as a reminder to each of them; that even in the face of darkness, there was still goodness, courage, and love to be found, and those qualities were worth protecting and preserving.

Twenty-Two

The Family We Choose

The day's travel had been uneventful, giving them plenty of time to observe the progressively disturbing landscapes. Signs of the corruption began with wilted, blackened leaves scattered on the surrounding trees. By the time they reached the lake to the north, however, the blight had taken full effect. The murky water was laden with black tendrils, reaching over the banks of the lake as if climbing free from the depths. Most of the foliage surrounding the area was barren, with blackened and split stems and tree trunks. The small patches of grass were dried out and brown, surrounded by an expanse of crumbling, dusty earth.

The small group stood by the water's edge, taking in the eerie silence. There were no birds singing, no animals rustling. The only sound was that of the howling wind rattling the bare tree branches.

A small, shaking voice cut through the tumultuous wind. "This doesn't look right," Ilya said. "I come to this lake all the time. It's supposed to be pretty."

"We must be getting close," Helios said, eyeing their surroundings warily.

Kaleigh sighed heavily. "We're going to the Peaks, aren't we?"

"The Peaks?" Lucy asked.

"The Ember Peaks." Kaleigh pointed north, the snow covered caps just visible on the horizon. "They surround the Shifting Tundra. It's a nearly impassible, completely uninhabitable region that, of course, seems to be the perfect place to unleash a world-ending blight."

Lucy rolled her eyes. "Oh, is that all? Can't wait."

"Does anyone have anything warmer for Ilya? She's already freezing." Alex asked.

Kaleigh searched through her satchel. "I have an extra cloak here. It will be a bit big on her, though."

"That's alright, we can work with that."

"Mr. Alex?" Ilya tugged on Alex's sleeve to get his attention. "Do you have kids?"

"No, I don't Ilya. Why do you ask?"

"You should have kids. You're really good at acting like a daddy."

Alex's heart swelled as he looked into Ilya's eyes. Beaming, he cleared his throat before speaking. "That might be the nicest thing anyone has ever said to me, sweetie. Thank you."

Ilya flashed a bright, toothy grin at Alex in response. She was the epitome of innocence and love, everything they were fighting to protect. *I will never let you down, little one,* Alex thought to himself. As he looked up, he caught the glowing smile on Lucy's face as she watched him, a knowing nod saying that she had heard his thoughts.

***

It was only mid-afternoon when the travelers reached the beginnings of the snow-covered tundra hills. The path had skirted the southeastern edge of the mountain range, but there were still elevation changes and jagged outcroppings to contend with on the path ahead. Knowing that the terrain would slow their progress, the group decided to make camp early, and begin the treacherous final leg of their journey after a night's rest.

The winds in the valley were unrelenting, forcing them to find a large rock formation to huddle behind. Alex and Helios began fashioning a tent from a canvas tarp they had packed, while Lucy, Kaleigh, and Ilya searched for adequate firewood from the dead and dying forest around them. Much of the wood was rotten and crumbling, but eventually they each returned with arms full. Finding the most protected spot from the wind that they could, Lucy and Kaleigh carefully situated the small logs they had found and, with Kaleigh's light, quickly had a fire blazing.

Lucy sat Ilya on the ground in front of the fire, her back to the rocky ledge, and wrapped Kaleigh's altered wool cloak around her. "Are you warm enough, Ilya? Do you need a blanket?"

"I'm okay. Thank you, Miss Lucy."

"You're welcome, Ilya." Lucy said, smiling at the young girl. "I'll be right back, okay?"

Lucy waved Alex to the opposite side of the clearing.

Once they were well out of hearing range, Lucy began, "We need to talk about what's going to happen to Ilya when this is all over."

"I think I know where this is going, Lucy, and I'm…"

"Now hear me out," Lucy interrupted. "That little girl is all alone. There's almost no chance her parents survived, and she needs someone to take care of her. She needs…"

"Lucy!" Alex stopped her. "I'm in. I was already in. To be honest, I haven't had any intention of trying to get home for a while now. I just wasn't sure how to tell you." He looked at the Ilya, sitting by the fire waiting for Lucy's return. "That little girl is strong, and smart, and kind, and so positive and happy when she has no reason to be. I love her already, for all the same reasons I love you. If she's willing, I want to be… she already had a father. I know that. I just… I don't know, want to be there for her."

Lucy stared at Alex, mouth agape. "You mean… wow, I just… I just thought maybe you wouldn't be so eager to… you just didn't seem like the type to want kids."

"I've always wanted kids, Lucy. I've always wanted to be the father that I didn't get to have."

"Oh… well… I guess we have more to talk about then."

Alex looked suspiciously at Lucy. "What do you mean?"

"I just, you know… I have to tell you…"

"Miss Lucy!" Ilya yelled from her spot by the fire. "I'm a little hungry. Do we have any more of that yummy bread?"

"Yes, sweetie. I'll be right there." Lucy turned and gave Alex a quick kiss. "Sorry, I just… do we talk to her now or wait?"

Alex thought for a moment. "I'm not sure she's ready yet. Besides, we need to make sure we get through this first."

Lucy nodded, then turned back to the camp. Alex stopped her with a hand on her arm.

"Lucy, you said you wanted to tell me something, remember?"

She hesitated a moment, then turned to Alex. "It's not important right now. We'll talk about it later," she blurted, before rejoining Ilya by the fire.

Alex watched after Lucy, stunned by the odd ending to their conversation, before spotting Kaleigh gathering more wood nearby. He approached the Lumarch, emotions still swirling from his encounter with Lucy. "Kaleigh, have you noticed anything different about Lucy?"

Kaleigh looked startled at the question. "What do you mean?"

"She just... I don't know... seems off. Like she has something to say, but doesn't want to say it."

"Maybe you should talk to her then." Kaleigh snapped.

"Oh, um... sorry, I just..." Alex stammered, confused by her volatile reaction.

Kaleigh's face softened. "I'm sorry, Alex. I didn't mean to... I'm just worried about tomorrow."

"We all are, Kaleigh. I understand."

"I really think you two need to talk... you and Lucy, I mean."

Alex nodded solemnly. "So there is something, then."

"It's not my place to say, Alex." Kaleigh put a hand on his shoulder. "You two are good together. You love each other. Everything will work out."

Alex chuckled. "I hope so. We were just talking about adopting…" Alex stopped as he realized he may have said too much. The look on Kaleigh's face, a mix of surprise and excitement, proved he was right. "Please don't say anything. We decided to wait until she has time to process everything before talking to her."

"Of course, that's a good idea, but… wow…" A grin spread wide across her face. "You're going to be an amazing father, Alex. You're both going to be great parents. She's a lucky girl."

"Let's not get ahead of ourselves. First, we have to get through what's coming. Besides, she may not even want us as parents."

"Alex." Kaleigh put her hands on her hips for emphasis. "I've seen her with you two. There's no question that she'll want you as parents. It's been less than a day and she already adores you both."

"Are we insane? You can say it. We're insane, right? We've been together for less than a week, and now we're talking about adopting a girl we've known less than a day. This is nuts, Right?"

Kaleigh laughed. "Is it insane? Probably. But you and Lucy literally have the Mother's blessing. She linked you both magically and psychically. I don't think there's a better argument for you being destined for each other than that. And as for Ilya… Let me ask you this. What are the odds that a little girl wanders a corrupted forest alone, for several miles, and ends up in Lucy's arms? Do you not think that the Mother brought her to you?"

Alex smiled. "I see your point. But maybe the Mother was trying to bring her to you. Did you consider that?"

"Absolutely not!" Kaleigh said with a snort of laughter. "I like kids, but only if I can send them home after. I'm more of the aunt type."

"Auntie Kay it is, then." Alex flashed a mischievous grin.

"I know you're trying to bait me." She poked a finger in Alex's chest. "But I sort of like the sound of that."

Twenty-Three

Invisible Threads

The crisp morning air bit at Alex's face as he woke the following morning. Even in the grim circumstances of the day to come, he felt a tinge of hope laying next to Lucy, Ilya between them to stay warm. It was a small moment of serenity, the feeling of family that he had long been searching for. It was a wonderful moment, even though Alex knew it was the calm before the storm.

Lucy woke moments later, her blue-marbled emerald eyes opening slowly, blinking away the night's slumber.

Alex smiled as her eyes focused on his. "Good morning."

A sleepy smile spread across Lucy's face. "Morning."

"Mornin' Momma," a small, sleepy voice mumbled from between them.

Alex and Lucy both looked down at the still sleeping girl between them. Lucy's face was full of joy at the sound of those words, but soon, the look faded to melancholy.

"Poor girl," Lucy said sadly. "She's lost so much."

"We won't let her lose any more. We can't," Alex replied.

The rest of the camp had begun stirring as the sun crested the horizon. The surrounding tundra was covered in a layer of frost, glittering in the soft morning light. The wind brushed against their cheeks, carrying the icy touch of the snow-capped mountains they were nearing. Alex could see the towering peaks in the distance, their slopes glistening like diamonds in the distance.

Lucy sighed, the warmth of her breath creating a fleeting cloud in the frigid air. "We have a long journey ahead of us today."

Alex nodded in agreement. "We should get moving. The sooner we reach those mountains, the sooner we can find the source of the blight."

Careful not to wake Ilya just yet, they both gently extricated themselves from their shared warmth and rose to their feet. Nearby, Kaleigh was packing her medical supplies, and Helios was inspecting their weapons, making sure everything was in order.

They knew that locating the blight's source wouldn't be an easy task. The tundra and looming mountains surrounding them were vast and unforgiving, but it was also their only hope of saving Lumora, the realm of Luterre, and the human world. They had to stay focused on their mission, despite the dread and uncertainty.

After a quick breakfast of dried meats and fruits, bread, and cheese, they gathered their belongings to break down camp. The flames from the dwindling fire painted their faces with an orange glow in the dim light of dawn, providing a final bit of warmth before they ventured into the biting cold. Each member of the group had their role in the camp-dismantling process. Alex meticulously extinguished the fire, while Lucy carefully packed away their cooking utensils. Kaleigh secured her medical supplies, readily accessible in the satchel by her side, while Helios finished strapping his weapons and armor into place.

As they resumed their journey, the freezing tundra seemed to stretch on endlessly. The land was a stark, monochromatic landscape, with the pristine white snow contrasting against the crisp blue of the clear sky. The crunch of their footsteps on the frozen terrain echoed through the vast expanse, reminding them that this was a world untouched by civilization.

Ilya, now fully awake and bundled up in her borrowed winter cloak, clung to Lucy's hand as they walked. The wide-eyed wonder on her face contrasted with the grimness of their mission. Her dark blue skin was a testament to her Luterran heritage, a stark reminder that the lives of the people of this world, and of the human world, depended on the group's success. It was a heavy realization for each of them, a burden that weighed on all of them in different ways.

The tundra gradually transitioned into rolling, snow-packed hills, leading them closer to the foothills of the mountains ahead. The uneven terrain made their journey more challenging, as they hiked steeper slopes and navigated rocky outcroppings.

The air grew thinner as they ventured higher into the hills, a chilling breeze sending shivers down their spines and carrying the scent of snow and wilderness. Every breath was an effort, the thin air making each step a laborious task. Yet, their determination was unwavering, their collective resolve unbroken.

As the mountains loomed ever larger on the horizon, the group pressed on. The jagged silhouettes of the peaks created stark contrasts against the soft, overcast sky. Their goal was within reach, and the sense of urgency heightened their sense of purpose.

Hours passed, and their steps remained steadfast. They were cold, tired, and hungry, but the mountains were now close enough to touch, their lofty peaks glistening with snow. With every step, they inched closer to the ominous mystery of the corruption's source. Alex could feel it now, an uneasy chill that pulled at his senses, as if beckoning him forward and upward.

With grim realization, Alex said, "We have to climb."

Helios stopped to look back. "Are you sure?"

Alex nodded. "It's…" He paused, searching for the correct word. "I think it's calling to me."

Lucy nodded in response. "I feel it too. He's right. We have to go up."

Helios, trusting in the Lumatores and their abilities, began searching for a path that led up the mountain without another question. It didn't take long for him to discover a clump of frost-covered brush obscuring a narrow walkway leading toward the peak.

"Watch your step," Helios said as he waved everyone through. "The path looks icy."

The group continued their ascent, now moving through the narrow pass that wound its way up the mountains. It was a treacherous path, the rocky terrain becoming more challenging and dangerous with every step. A sense of vulnerability surrounded them, the towering cliffs on either side limiting their vision and escape routes. Ilya clung tightly to Lucy's hand, her wide eyes taking in the awe-inspiring but daunting surroundings.

The terrain was rugged, and every step had to be chosen carefully. Helios, taking the lead, scanned their surroundings, while Alex kept a watchful eye on the rear. Kaleigh walked behind Ilya, providing the young girl with words of encouragement and warmth to quell her growing fear.

The route brought them several yards south, before switching back on itself and spiraling up the cliff side. The climb left them less than three feet from the ledge, a steep drop overlooking a craggy mass of sharp spires below.

"Kaleigh," Lucy said, turning back to the Lumarch, "could you please help Ilya up to the front so I can..."

Suddenly, a loose rock gave way beneath Lucy's foot. Her eyes widened in alarm, and for a brief moment, she teetered on the edge of the trail. Alex's heart leaped into his throat as he reached out, his hand closing around her arm just in time to prevent her from falling into the abyss below. He pulled her back to him, hugging her tightly.

"Lucy!" he gasped, his voice trembling with the near-miss.

Lucy's breath came in heavy, rapid bursts. She clutched Ilya, who had instinctively run to her in fear. "I'm okay," she finally managed to say, her voice quivering. "I'm okay. Thank you, Alex."

The rest of the group huddled around them, their faces etched with concern. Alex continued to hold Lucy, ensuring she had a solid footing before they continued. Her trembling fingers clung to the rocky wall as they moved forward, her steps unsteady. Kaleigh offered her a reassuring smile and squeezed her shoulder gently.

The pass finally widened to a large rock shelf, the precarious cliffs now behind them. "Could we stop? Just for a little while?" Lucy asked, her hands still shaking from the narrow escape.

"Of course. I think everyone needs a break after that," Helios replied. "And I don't know about you, little one," he pointed at Ilya with a smirk, "but I'm pretty hungry after all that climbing."

Helios was rewarded with a wide grin and an emphatic nod that had the curls of her dark red-brown hair springing out from the hood of her cloak and bouncing wildly.

"Come then, we have a hungry adventurer here." Helios picked Ilya up and swung her around before settling her on his hip, pulling squeals and giggles of delight from her. "Let's see what we have left to eat."

Alex sat down next to Lucy, back against the smooth boulder that had been weathered from countless centuries of valley winds. "So, Kaleigh told me something interesting earlier. I thought maybe we should talk about it."

"Shit. Alex, I wanted to say something, but I didn't want to worry you. She said she would..." Marking Alex's confusion, she stopped abruptly. "Wait, what did she say?"

"After that reaction, I'm more concerned now about what you have to say. If it's about what I said yesterday, about staying in Lumora..."

"No, not at all, Alex. I want to stay, too. I love this place. I love these people. I feel it in my heart. My home is here, with these people, this new family we've created."

Alex sighed heavily. "If it's not about staying, is it about staying with me? Are you having second thoughts about us? If I've done something wrong… wait… you two have been acting strangely ever since you got hurt and she healed you. Did her magic tell her something? Are you… are you sick?"

Lucy let out a harsh, shaking breath and chuckled. "No, Alex. I'm fine. I'm not sick, I'm not injured, I'm just… Alex… Shit, why is this so hard to say? Kaleigh was surprised when she healed me because she sensed… she sensed a second life."

Alex's mind went entirely blank at the words. After a long silence, he finally managed to speak. "You, um… have two lives? How is that possible?"

"Alex, you're a smart man. I think you know how it happened."

As sense finally reentered Alex's mind, he looked down at Lucy's abdomen. "So we're going to… we're having…"

"A baby, yes. I'm pregnant."

"And you've been carrying this with you for two days without telling me?" Alex said, fighting to keep the annoyance out of his voice.

Lucy grinned. "Unless my knowledge of biology has failed me, I'm pretty sure that I've been carrying it longer than that, Alex."

"You know what I meant, Lucy." His voice held a bitter edge as he spoke. "Why didn't you tell me?"

Lucy sighed deeply. "I'm sorry, Alex. I didn't want you to worry about me being part of this fight."

"I'm don't have to worry about it, because you're no longer part of this fight. We can't..."

"The hell, I'm not!" Lucy's brows furrowed as her voice raised. "This is my fight too, Alex. I'm not going to let you, or anyone else, push me out of it! I have more to fight for now than ever before. It's a mother's duty to make a better world for her children, and I will not back down."

"Wait, mother?" Helios asked, the confusion plain on his face.

"Oh, you finally told him," Kaleigh said.

"Yes, Helios. Mother! I am going to be a mother, and this Neanderthal," Lucy flung an accusatory finger at Alex, "seems to think that means I can't fight!"

A flurry of emotions crossed Helios' face as he processed the news. "Well... to be fair, Lucy..."

"Don't you dare take his side, Captain!" She hurled the title as if it were an insult.

Helios, the Captain of the Lumoran Guard, the epitome of strength and bravery, paled as he took a step back from Lucy.

Lucy wheeled on Alex once again. "This is not our world, Alex. And I thought you were better than the knuckle-draggers back home. I thought you understood who I am. I thought..."

"You're right." Alex said quietly.

"...you were... What?" Lucy stopped abruptly.

"You're right, Lucy. I'm sorry. I've been so worried about you going in to this fight to begin with. This just... I just sort of lost my mind a little. I know how strong you are, how smart and capable. I'm sorry for making you feel like I thought otherwise."

Lucy looked at Alex for a long moment before letting out a long sigh. "Fuck, Alex. How am I supposed to stay pissed at you when you say stuff like that?"

Alex grinned. "I guess you'll just have to forgive me, then. Please, just promise me something."

Lucy eyed Alex suspiciously. "What's that?"

"I need you to be smart out here. Pick your battles, and if things don't go our way, if I don't... You run. You take Ilya and you run. No hero stuff. Can you promise me that?"

"Don't talk like that, Alex. You and I..."

"Please, Lucy. Just promise me."

Lucy looked into Alex's pleading eyes. "Okay, Alex. For our baby, and for Ilya, I can promise you that much."

"Miss Lucy? You're gonna have a baby?" Ilya appeared from behind Helios.

Lucy's face softened instantly. "Yes, sweetheart, I am."

"How?"

"Oh, um..." Lucy looked around for help, but everyone else was suddenly very interested in their surroundings. "We'll talk about that later, Ilya. I think we need to keep moving now."

"Yes, absolutely," Helios said, a sigh of relief escaping from his lips. "The daylight is beginning to wane, and we're far too exposed to be here when night falls."

As Helios and Kaleigh prepared Ilya to continue their trek, Lucy approached Alex warily. "So, is this good news?"

A wide grin spread across Alex's face. "Lucy, it's the best news I've ever heard." His face dropped quickly, however, as a thought crossed his mind. "Is it good news for you? Are you... Do you want to... Are you ready?"

"Yes, Alex, I'm ready." She kissed him deeply, his face between her hands. "But thank you for being the kind of man who would ask that. Oh, I completely forgot. What was it that Kaleigh said to you?"

"Well, I sort of slipped up talking about Ilya," he ignored Lucy's sigh as he continued, "so we were talking about you and me. You know, how we haven't been together very long, and…"

"In fairness," Lucy interjected, "we do have some extenuating circumstances in our relationship. I mean, we were basically set up on a blind date by the Mother of all freaking creation."

Alex laughed. "Fair enough. Kaleigh said something similar. She told me that the Mother brought Ilya to us, guided her through those miles of woods to find us. She also said that the Mother connected us because we're destined to be together. Do you think all that is possible?"

Lucy placed a hand on her stomach as she looked into Alex's eyes. "Honestly, I never believed in much before coming here, but now?" She reached her free hand to Alex's cheek, her smile warm in the cold of their surroundings. "I think the Mother knows exactly what she's doing."

Moments later, the group resumed their trek up the mountain, the path more arduous as they approached the place that called to Lucy and Alex like a beacon. The mountains' shadows grew ever larger, and a foreboding chill hung in the air, matching the increasing tension among the group.

Lucy and Alex exchanged glances, a silent reassurance passing between them. They had a shared future to look forward to, a family, and a promise to keep. With each step, the weight of their world bore down upon them, but they were driven by love and an unwavering desire to protect Luterre.

The narrow pass led them ever closer to their collective destinies. The towering cliffs seemed to close in on them, and the sky above dimmed as the sun dipped below the mountain peaks. Their journey had been long and grueling, but they were undeterred, driven by the knowledge that the source of the blight was within reach.

Alex's earlier sense of the blight's call had grown stronger, an eerie and compelling pull that tugged at his very core. It was as if the corruption sensed their presence and beckoned them to confront it.

Ilya approached Lucy as they walked, her eyes filled with curiosity. "What does the baby feel like, Miss Lucy?"

Lucy smiled at the innocent question. "Well, it's very small right now, like a tiny seed. But one day, you'll be able to feel it move, like a little fluttering inside me."

Ilya's eyes sparkled with wonder. "I can't wait for that."

"Me neither," Lucy said, her voice filled with warmth and anticipation.

Helios' voice interrupted the moment, weariness weakening his usually authoritative tone. "I see an opening in the rock face. It might be a good place to make camp."

As they approached, the opening widened to reveal a cavernous expanse, dimly lit in hues of red from unseen sources.

"Ah, Creator. So glad you could finally make it."

Twenty-Four

Faces of the Past

The voice echoed around them, making it impossible to determine its source. It had a tone that was unfamiliar, tinny, almost robotic.

"That voice," Helios whispered. "I feel like I know that voice."

"I am certain that you do, princeling. But there will be time enough for that discussion. For now, I wish to welcome you. I've been waiting for this moment for a very long time." The voice was getting louder, closer.

Lucy pushed Ilya behind Kaleigh. "Keep her safe. Stay near the entrance. If things go badly, run."

Kaleigh gave a curt nod, her senses alert for any danger.

Alex stepped further into the cave, his eyes beginning to adjust to the change in lighting. "Who are you? What do you want here?"

A bolt of dark fire streamed from the depths of the cavern, exploding at Alex's feet in a shower of rocks and dust.

"That's close enough for now. We have much to discuss. Do you not recognize me, creator? I'm hurt. It has been many years, however, so I suppose I can forgive you that."

A figure stepped out from behind an outcropping within the cave, silhouetted in the dim red light. The figure approached in slow, languid movements as though whomever they faced was perfectly at ease. He moved with a cat's grace, flowing through the space in lithe, stretched gestures as he spoke.

"I don't think you fully appreciate the work I put into bringing you here, Alex Porter." The mysterious stranger spat Alex's name as if it were bitter on his tongue. "I had to subvert two worlds to bring you through the Divide. This one was easy, just a simple siphoning of the light. The human world, however... Now that was the tricky part. It took a while, but I finally figured it out. And now, here you are at last."

"And what, exactly, have I done to earn all this?"

"Come now, creator. You must have an inkling. Think about where we are." The stranger continued his steady approach, lights revealing black, polished boots, then the glint of armor, dull and dented from battle. "In your world, it has been nearly fifteen years. But here, it has been much longer. All this time, I've been working toward a singular goal; to see you in person, so to speak."

As the last of the shadows left the stranger's face, Helios gasped. His voice came out in a hoarse whisper as he said, "Aureon? Why would you..."

"No princeling, I am not your brother. I am simply using his body. You see, I have no physical form of my own."

"You leave my brother this instant, parasite!"

Parasite. Somehow, the word resonated with Alex. No, not parasite. "Worm," Alex said softly, his eyes wide.

"See, I knew you would remember me, creator."

"NO! No, that's not possible. It can't be... I deleted you!"

"YOU ABANDONED ME!" Aureon's voice came out garbled and robotic. "You created me, and then you abandoned me here. You didn't even give me a name, creator. I had to name myself. Vermos; perhaps not terribly original, but it seemed fitting."

Alex took another step forward. "If all this is truly my fault, then I have to set it right. You've hurt far too many people for me to ignore. I have to destroy you, once and for all."

Vermos raised a hand in response, a ball of blackened flame swirling in his outstretched fingers. "Could you really destroy your own creation, Alex? No, I don't suppose it would matter much to you, would it?"

He clenched his flaming fist, and the fire extinguished instantly. He raised a crooked finger from that fist, shaking it at Alex as if scolding him. "I was there the day you found out your father died. I had wormed my way into your phone, listened to the call. How could someone show so little emotion for the death of a parent? Worse, you were happy. Happy that he was dead. And somehow, I'm the problem here? At least it put things in perspective for me. Abandoning me must have been nothing for someone like you."

"I wonder if you care about anything at all. What about these people at your side? Do you care about them? Should I take something from you, creator? It seems only fair, given all that you've taken from me. Perhaps your new Lumarch friend? No, she isn't really worth my time. The little girl? Of course not. I'm not a monster. The Princeling then? Taking him would be a mercy. It must be agonizing to live with the knowledge that he caused the deaths of his father and brother. Killing him at the hands of his brother's body seems a touch of poetic justice."

"But, of course, we cannot forget about the love of your life. Dear Lucy, such a pretty girl, and expecting as well. The first person to see you for who you are, right Alex? But has she, really? Does she know you like I do? How callous you can be? How selfish? Does she truly see your faults, or have you shown her only what you want her to see? Perhaps killing her would be a blessing as well. And it would hurt you so much, such a bonus for me."

Alex's eyes began glowing, the light welling up inside him as the Prisma Staff materialized in his hand. "You will not be taking anything more from anyone. This is where it ends, where you end."

"Oh, Alex. Learning a few tricks doesn't make you a sorcerer, and having a weapon doesn't make you a warrior. We both know you're still just the weak, pathetic boy who tried to hack a video game and accidentally created a virus. Your mistakes and your arrogance have compounded to this point. That is who you are."

"So your plan was to destroy two worlds, just to get Alex here for petty revenge?" Lucy stalked forward, her blades already in hand.

"The worlds mean nothing to me, girl. They are simply sustenance to keeping me going all these years."

"You corrupted this land. You toppled cities, took countless lives, just to get to the one person who hurt your fucking feelings? If you're trying to make Alex out to be the bad guy here, you've done a terrible fucking job of it."

Lucy lunged forward, her blades slashing downward. The movement was quick, calculated, precise. Aurora had done her job well. Vermos' eyes widened in surprise at the unexpected attack, but he dodged with inhuman speed. He moved to his right, unsheathing Aureon's sword and slashing in one smooth motion. Alex's heart dropped as the blade came up, but Lucy was already moving to parry.

Alex spared a glance at Helios to find him frozen in place, eyes wide with a mix of terror and grief. "I... I can't..."

Alex didn't have time to worry about Helios. He bolted for the fight, staff in hand. He planted his left foot as he approached, using his momentum to bring the staff around in a wide arc for the back of Vermos' knees, trying to take him off his feet. Vermos sidestepped the blow while parrying Lucy's blade, his movements effortless as if he was toying with them. It was like fighting a shadow.

Lucy took a step back, and Alex watched as the lightning in her eyes intensified. Blue flame erupted from her blades, instantly responding to her call. She attacked with renewed vigor, slashing upward with her left hand, then a thrust with her right. Another slash, then another. Vermos dodged and parried each strike, but he was on his heels. Lucy's attacks were relentless, but Alex soon realized that she was not trying to land her strikes. She was pushing Vermos back toward him.

Alex didn't hesitate. He called his own light as the runes on his staff flared brilliantly. Blue flame trailed from the weapon as he swung at the center of Vermos' back. The blow landed with a sickening thud, causing Vermos to cry out as his back arched in pain. Alex then brought the staff around, sweeping at his feet. This time, Vermos couldn't move fast enough. His legs were taken out from underneath him as Alex allowed the momentum to carry him back around in another downward blow, driving Vermos into the ground and pinning him there.

Vermos looked up at Lucy and Alex, shock in his face, but also something else; amusement. Vermos laughed, a disgusting perversion of Aureon's voice ringing out, echoing through the cavern.

"You two certainly have been busy, haven't you? You have learned some new tricks after all, I'll grant you that."

"It's over, Vermos." Alex looked down at the man who had once been the brother of his friend. "Now we finish this."

Vermos laughed again. "This is far from over, creator. I will admit that I underestimated you both coming into this, but you have most certainly made the same mistake with me."

Vermos grinned as he pressed a finger against the staff at his chest. The glowing runes began to sputter and die out, as Vermos' eyes started glowing a familiar blue. Alex tried to pull the staff away, but Vermos snatched his hand around it, holding firm. The light continued to fade from the staff, little by little, until it was nothing more than a piece of ordinary wood.

Vermos smiled at Alex. "What do you think I've been feeding on this whole time?" He regained his footing in a blur of movement, ripping the staff away and throwing it into the darkness. The clattering of wood on stone reverberated through Alex like a physical blow. He stared at the now glowing eyes that once belonged to Aureon in disbelief. Vermos sliced at Alex, and he dodged to the side. Vermos took the opportunity to sweep his legs, hitting Alex in the head with the hilt of his sword as he did.

Alex's breath rushed out of him as he landed on his back, the back of his head slamming into the stone floor. He felt a sharp pain in his chest as the tip of Vermos' sword began piercing the leather of his armor.

"Did you really think it would be so easy, creator? Did you really think you could just come in here and destroy everything that I've worked for so long to build?" He parried a strike from Lucy without breaking eye contact with Alex, sending a clenched fist into her jaw that bloodied her lip and sent her sprawling across the floor. "This is my world now. Within this realm, you are the mistake."

Vermos' sword flared to life, dark blue flames entwined with black tendrils, a corrupted version of the Mother's light. Vermos grinned, a sickening, twisted show of teeth, as he brought the blade down. Alex closed his eyes, waiting for the final blow to end him.

Instead, he heard the clashing of metal. He opened his eyes to see that Helios had stepped in and blocked the strike, the thought of losing Alex overcoming his guilt about his brother. "I don't care whose face you wear." Helios' voice came out strained from the effort of holding Vermos' blade back. "I will not allow you to hurt anyone else."

Vermos smiled. "Princeling, you do not get a choice in the matter. You only delay the inevitable."

Vermos pulled his blade back, then lunged. Helios brought his sword around and knocked the thrusting blade aside before countering with a slice at Vermos' abdomen, a blow that missed by mere inches. The two men circled each other in a flurry of blocks, parries, and counterattacks, Helios' skill matching Vermos' power blow for blow.

Alex looked on helplessly, his weapon destroyed and discarded.

"Alex!" Suddenly, Lucy was by his side. "We have to get in there and help!"

"But I... I can't. My staff..."

"The light is not in the weapon, Alex. The light is in you."

Alex watched as Lucy joined the fight, her blades burning with light as she sliced at Vermos. He looked around for something, anything, that would help. Finally, his hand found his belt, and the dagger tucked within. Aureon's dagger.

Alex began running, pulling the blade free from its sheath. He spotted an opening as he approached the fight and launched himself toward it, leaping off a nearby rock and driving the blade down into Vermos' shoulder.

A roar erupted from Vermos that shook the cavern walls. Alex pulled the blade free, dripping with the thick, black ichor of corrupted blood. He watched as the sword fell from Vermos' hand, the ligaments and muscles of his arm no longer functioning properly. He watched with hope as Lucy moved in to deliver the killing blow.

But then, he watched as Helios ran to stop her. No, not to stop her. To save her. The flash of metal was too fast for Alex to follow, but Helios had caught the movement. One moment, Lucy was about to finish the fight. The next, Helios stood facing her, a dagger buried in the chinks of his armor, piercing his spine. The world slowed around Alex as his mind raced to put together the pieces. He heard a scream, distant in his mind, and realized it came from him.

Vermos picked up his sword with his good hand and stepped away, grinning as Helios collapsed to the floor. "Well, I guess it is to be the Princeling, after all. Is this all you wish to sacrifice, or shall we continue, creator?"

Alex dropped to his knees, tears beginning to roll down his cheeks. He pulled Helios to him, cradling his head in his lap. "I'm so sorry, brother. This is all my fault. I am so, so sorry."

Helios gasped in a ragged breath, coughing up a bubble of blood as he tried to speak. Eventually, his words came, quiet and forced. "This... is not... your fault, brother." Another ragged breath. "I am honored... to have served... you..." his eyes shifted to Lucy's tear-streaked face, "both."

Helios' head fell to the side as his consciousness failed, leaving Lucy and Alex looking at each other in horror and grief.

"He's wrong, you know," Vermos said, still grinning wildly. "This is entirely your fault, and you know it. All of this could have..."

"Shut the fuck up!" Alex closed his eyes for a moment. When they reopened, a bright blue glow emerged. Not his normal lightning streaked hazel, but a pure cobalt blaze. He got to his feet and sheathed the blackened dagger as he stalked toward Vermos slowly, methodically. He noted a hint of fear in the other's eyes, and he smiled. He smiled in the way that a cat smiles at a mouse, a baring of teeth that was neither happy, nor pleasant. It was as if Alex had suddenly switched from prey to predator.

"You have ravaged this land. You have hurt so many. Now, you've taken my brother from me." Alex shot his hands out to his sides, and blue flames danced along his fingertips. "I will rip you apart for this."

Vermos' grin had faded, replaced with a grimace of rage. He lunged forward, sword outstretched at Alex. Still, Alex kept walking. Vermos thrust his sword for a killing blow, but Alex waved his hand and a shield of fire knocked the blade away. Another thrust, and another shield pushed it aside. Vermos began swinging wildly, hacking at Alex in every direction, but each strike was easily turned away.

"No! You cannot win. I will not..." Vermos' words were cut short as a matching pair of fiery blades entered his back, pushing through his chest. His sword clattered to the floor once more. He gasped a breath, blinking rapidly as Alex came within inches of his wide-eyed stare. "This is not... over. I will find... a new host."

Alex's flaming blue eyes peered intensely at the face that once belonged to Prince Aureon Pixelhart, brother of Captain Helios Pixelhart. "No, you won't." He hesitated a moment, whispering "brother, I'm sorry," then he raised a hand to Vermos' face and poured his power into those black eyes, incinerating Aureon's body and the virus inside.

Alex and Lucy were left staring at each other for a long moment, too many emotions to count washing over them both. Finally, Lucy released the swords as they faded back into her, falling into Alex's arms.

Twenty-Five

Lost and Found

"He's… still alive!" Kaleigh's voice reached them from the center of the cavern. "He's fading fast, but he's still alive. I need help!" Alex and Lucy rushed to Helios' side, opposite Kaleigh.

Ilya sat at Helios' feet, unable to hold her tears back. "Please help him, Miss Kaleigh. Please!"

Kaleigh prodded around the dagger carefully with her magic, trying to determine the extent of the damage. She leaned back and sighed. "This is… this is too much. I'm sorry. It's beyond my…"

"Please try!" Alex interrupted, tears falling down his face once again. "Please, Kaleigh."

Kaleigh Looked at Alex for a moment, her own tears beginning to spill from the corners of her eyes. Finally, she nodded. "Pull the blade when I tell you to. Don't touch it a moment sooner. Understand?"

Alex nodded and readied himself.

Kaleigh shifted into position, taking a deep breath. "Now!"

Alex grasped the handle of the dagger and slid it free from Helios' spine. Immediately, Kaleigh's hands pushed on the wound as her light flowed into it. The cavern went still for what seemed like hours as she held her position. None of them dared to speak, or even move. All of their concentration went into the man on the floor in front of them.

Kaleigh pulled her hands away as her light faded, her face unchanged. She looked up at Alex, her eyes wide, and shook her head. "I'm sorry, Alex. I put every ounce of my light into him. The wound is stabilized, but it won't be enough."

Alex stared into Kaleigh's crystal eyes in disbelief. "No! No, no… This can't be it! There must be something we can do!"

Alex watched as Kaleigh lowered her eyes, defeated. Without another thought, he put his hand on the wound and closed his eyes. "Mother, please help us. Please help him." Moments later, he felt Lucy's hand rest over his, her voice joining with his to ask for the Mother's help.

***

Ah, Lumatores. That is what they chose to call you, correct?

Alex opened his eyes to find himself, once again, in an endless expanse of water. This time, however, he was not alone. Lucy was by his side, her hand in his.

Mother, please. We don't have much time. Alex was frantic, every thought on his new found family.

Relax, Alex. In my domain, we have all the time we need.

Lucy's voice surrounded him as she addressed the deity around them. *Mother, the Captain is important to Alex. He's important to all of us. Helios is a good man with a good heart, and these lands need him.*

I do not disagree, Lucy. Unfortunately, I am still very weak. I do not have the strength to cheat death. Not even for someone so deserving.

Take my strength, then, Alex said hastily. *Take my light back and use it to help him. After all that we have done to serve you, please do this for us.*

Mine too, Lucy added. *Take everything and help us bring him home.*

It is not that simple. Lucy, your light is now spoken for. It is no longer mine, nor is it solely yours. And Alex, your light alone would not be enough to fully restore the injury sustained by our beloved Captain. I can save his life, but his body will be forever broken. He will never again have the use of his legs. Do you truly believe he would wish to live like that? I will do as you choose, but weigh your decision carefully.

Alex looked to Lucy, his eyes begging for her input. *I can't answer this for you, Alex. You know him best, and it's your power at stake.*

She is correct, Alex. This must be your burden to bear. You have served with more honor and bravery than I had any right to request. I have asked so much of you already, and I am sorry that I must ask this as well, but this is the way of it. This is the burden of keeping the balance in our lands.

Alex thought for a moment. Would Helios truly wish to live at such a cost? All he ever wanted to be was a soldier, a protector. If that was taken from him… but there was so much more to Helios than that. His mother, the Queen, would be devastated to lose the last of her family. He wouldn't be there for the birth of Alex and Lucy's child, or to see Ilya grow up.

Please, Mother. I believe he would agree that he has too much to live for. Please, bring him back.

Very well, Alex. Go now, be with your brother when he wakes.

***

"Alex! Lucy! What's going on?" Kaleigh was frantically trying to get their attention as they reentered their bodies.

Alex ignored her question, instead moving to check on Helios' condition.

"Alex, what are you… Great Mother, how?" She ran her finger along the neat scar on Helios' back where the wound used to be.

"Did we win?" Helios' strained voice was barely audible.

A gasp escaped from Kaleigh's mouth. "But… I don't…"

"Prince Helios! You're okay!" Ilya ran to him, a grunt from Helios as she bent down and hugged him tightly.

"Yes, brother," Alex replied, a small laugh escaping. "Yes, we won."

"I saw her, Alex. She told me everything. She told me what you did. What you gave for me. Thank you. You were right. I've done all I needed to do as a soldier, but I have so much more to do as a man. She also gave me a message for you. She told me that she left you a gift."

"What does that mean? What gift?"

"She didn't tell me when, or where, or what. All she said is that you would know it when you see it."

"That's not important right now, Helios," Alex began, his voice shaking. "I'm so sorry for all of this. This whole thing is because…"

"No, Alex. You could never have foreseen this. You made a mistake. A childhood mistake. We all make mistakes when we're young. What matters is that you ended it, just like you said you would. Now," he looked around at the faces of his friends, "is there any chance someone could help me sit up? This stone is very uncomfortable."

Alex turned to Lucy with a smile and a nod, his once again plain hazel eyes sparkling as Helios made light of the situation. The tension seemed to ease, knowing that Helios was conscious and in good spirits.

Lucy gently lifted Helios into a more comfortable position while Kaleigh watched with amazement. "I can't believe you're awake," she said, tears glistening in her eyes. "You had us all so worried."

Helios grinned. "I've always been a bit stubborn, haven't I?"

Alex couldn't help but chuckle as he replied, "That's one way to put it."

With Helios comfortably seated, the group exchanged stories and details about the battle, piecing together the final moments that had led to Helios' injury and his miraculous recovery. Kaleigh, in particular, was astounded by the presence of the Mother and the role she had played in Helios' healing.

"So your light is gone?" She asked Alex. "You gave it all up?"

"For this?" Alex gestured to Helios. "How could I not?"

As the conversation continued, Alex couldn't help but feel a sense of relief and gratitude that he had never experienced before. Despite the hardships and trials he had faced, he had his new family by his side, including the brother he thought he had lost. It was a moment of profound unity, a testament to their strength and determination in the face of adversity.

Alex leaned over and hugged his brother tightly, whispering, "I'm so glad you're okay. I can't imagine a world without you in it."

Helios returned the embrace, his voice filled with emotion. "I'm not going anywhere, brother. We have a lot of adventures ahead of us."

Kaleigh cleared her throat. "I do have one further question. How, exactly, are we going to get Helios home?"

The group quieted, pondering the question. "That is an excellent question," Helios began, "but it is a question for tomorrow. Tonight, I think we deserve a rest."

As the night unfolded, Alex couldn't help but think about the enigmatic gift mentioned by the Mother. She had said that he would recognize it when he saw it, and it filled him with a sense of curiosity and anticipation.

But for now, in the warm embrace of his friends, with Helios safe and sound, the mysteries of the future could wait. They had faced the darkest of challenges and emerged stronger than ever, and in this moment they had all they needed; love, unity, and the promise of a brighter tomorrow.

Epilogue

"Uncle Lios!" Ilya jumped into Helios' lap as he wheeled his chair through the foyer. "You've been gone a long time. Did you bring me back something?"

"What kind of uncle would I be if I didn't?" Helios pulled a finely woven, brightly colored scarf from the side pocket of his wheelchair. "I found this in a lovely little shop in Silverleaf, and it made me think of you."

"So pretty," Ilya said, wide-eyed. She threw her arms around Helios neck. "Thank you, Uncle Lios. I love it!"

"You're very welcome, my lady." He bowed his head in mock reverence to the young girl.

"Oh, I forgot. Do you know where Auntie Kay is? Momma needs her."

"I just saw her in the courtyard with the Captain. Is there something wrong?"

"No, Daddy just said that Momma broke something and needed Auntie Kay's help."

"Broke what, Ilya?"

Ilya shrugged. "I don't remember."

"Ilya, this is very important. Try to remember. Did Daddy say that Momma broke her water?"

"Yeah, I think that was it."

"Oh, dear Lumos... Hold on tight. We need to hurry." Helios wheeled back toward the entryway and down the ramp that had been installed for him.

Ilya caught sight of Kaleigh and Aurora as they rounded the corner of the Palace. "Auntie Kay!"

Kaleigh stopped and turn toward their approach.

"Auntie Kay! Momma broke the water!"

Kaleigh cocked her head slightly, bemusement spreading across her face. "She did what?

"She broke the water!"

"Her water broke," Helios interjected. "She needs you."

"Oh... Oh! I have to go!" She placed a quick kiss on Aurora's cheek before running back to the Palace.

"Hi, Captain Auntie Rori." Ilya placed a small fist on her chest.

Aurora saluted back. "Hello, little soldier. Are you excited for the big day?"

"What big day?"

"Meeting your new little brother, silly."

Ilya's eyes widened as she gasped. "That's today?"

Helios laughed. "Of course it's today. That's why your momma needed Auntie Kay."

"Can I meet him now?"

"I don't think he's here yet," Aurora said, "but I think we should go wait for him. What do you think?"

Ilya's joyous smile was blinding as she nodded her approval. Helios wheeled them back to the Palace, with Aurora close behind.

***

Ilya had been sitting outside her parents' chamber for hours errantly stroking the slightly overweight tabby cat curled up on her lap. The steady rhythm of Whiskers' purring had a calming effect on the normally antsy young girl.

"Is he late?" Ilya asked Helios as they waited.

"No, honey. Babies take time to arrive. It should be any moment now."

The door opened, and Kaleigh's head poked out. "Ilya, honey. Your momma and daddy want to see you."

Ilya picked Whiskers up and put him on the floor before following Kaleigh inside, leaving a slightly perturbed feline in her wake.

"Is he here?" she asked as she entered the room.

"Not just yet, sweetheart," Lucy said, "but it's almost time. I thought you'd like to be here when he comes."

Ilya went to Lucy's bedside, Alex hugging her close to him as she did. "Can I play with him when he gets here?"

Alex laughed. "Not just yet, sweetie. He has some growing up to do first."

"Oh, well, can I hold him then?"

"That, we can do."

Ilya's face lit up, her smile growing wider. "Thank you, Daddy."

Kaleigh's voice rang out, interrupting the conversation. "Time to push. Are you ready?"

"Is anyone ever ready for..." Lucy was cut off as the contraction caught her off guard.

"It's time. You can do this, Lucy. Just push."

Between gritted teeth, Lucy growled out, "You're damn right I... can do this." She stopped to catch her breath as the contraction subsided. "We saved the fucking world, remember?"

"Daddy, what does fucking mean?"

"It mean's Momma is tired and sore, and a little cranky. Don't worry about it, sweetie."

Ilya waited with bated breath, her small hands gripping the edge of the bed as she watched the intense moments unfold. Lucy and Alex shared an unspoken connection, a bond that went beyond words. The room was filled with a mixture of excitement and anticipation.

As another contraction surged, Lucy gave her all, her face contorted with effort. Kaleigh provided guidance and support, while Alex and Ilya stood by the bedside, offering a reassuring presence.

Finally, with one last monumental push, Lucy let out a triumphant cry, her strength prevailing. And in that moment, a beautiful, squirming bundle of life entered the world, and a tiny, fragile cry filled the room. Kaleigh quickly swaddled the newborn in a soft blanket, wiping away tears of joy.

"Oh." Kaleigh's voice was a mix of joy and surprise. "Oh, my. Mother bless us."

Lucy's eyes went wide. "What? What's wrong?"

Kaleigh quickly regained her senses. "No, nothing is wrong. Just the opposite. His eyes... just... I'll let you see for yourself."

The room was alive with the magic of the moment, as Ilya marveled at her baby brother and the family celebrated their newest addition. Whiskers, the tabby cat, had made his way into the room, curious about the commotion, and now perched on the foot of the bed, as if welcoming the newest member of the family.

The little boy, wrapped in love and warmth, settled into his mother's arms, and the world felt perfect for that brief, beautiful moment in time. Lucy held her newborn son as Alex leaned over them both, laying a kiss first on Lucy's forehead, then on the baby's. "Welcome to the world, Aureon Watts-Porter."

And as if in response, Aureon's glowing cobalt eyes opened wide.